THE HANGING

They continued in silence. All round her, Willow smelt a familiar juicy yet metallic odour. She knew she was crossing the garlic once again – the ring of garlic.

Behind her, she heard Blue muttering in his sleep. "*It keeps the evil out!*" he whispered. "*It keeps the evil in!*"

Like everyone else, Willow knew that a ring of garlic – wild garlic – was supposed to keep vampires, hobgoblins and ghouls at bay. An unbroken chain would not allow any evil to pass through. But what if the rhyme was right? What if the ring of garlic could enclose the evil, locking it up within its embrace?

Willow gasped. The four of them were now inside that circle themselves...

Have you read?

Blood Sinister
The Vanished
Celia Rees

Transformer
Philip Gross

The Carver
Jenny Jones

At Gehenna's Door
Peter Beere

House of Bones
Graham Masterson

Look out for:

Catchman
Chris Wooding

THE HANGING TREE

Paul Stewart

SCHOLASTIC

Scholastic Children's Books,
Commonwealth House, 1-19 New Oxford Street,
London WC1A 1NU, UK
a division of Scholastic Ltd
London ~ New York ~ Toronto ~ Sydney ~ Auckland

First published in the UK by Scholastic Ltd, 1998

ISBN 0 590 11164 7

Typeset by
Cambrian Typesetters, Frimley, Camberley, Surrey
Printed by Cox and Wyman Ltd, Reading, Berks.

10 9 8 7 6 5 4 3 2 1

For Joseph

1

Willow shuddered for the third time in as many minutes. She looked up nervously from the pot of soup she was stirring, and squinted into the tree above her. Something felt wrong.

"Are you OK up there, Gary?" she called.

"Yep!" came the reply. "I've cut the main platform to the right shape. Now, all I've got to do is fix it into place. Shouldn't take me long."

The shudders persisted. "Well, just take care," she said, louder than she'd intended. Gary heard her.

"Right you are, Mother," he shouted back.

Willow blushed, but smiled. She liked Gary, even when he teased her. He was one of those people who managed to be both efficient and laid-back.

Unlike her mum, who was neither. Despite the crystals Sara clutched, the incense she burned and the herbal teas she drank, she was always twitchy and on edge. She was also the most impractical person in the world.

For a start, she was the one who had wanted to set up camp in the shadow of the ancient oak tree. Willow had hated the place immediately. It was dark and creepy. But her mum had been adamant. "It's perfect!" she exclaimed. "The shafts of sunlight. The dappled forest floor. This magnificent tree..."

"It's also swarming with mosquitoes," said Willow.

"Oh, a couple of insects won't hurt you," she said. "Anyway, I've got some citronella in my bag. That'll keep them away."

"Family vote," Willow demanded.

Of course, the outcome had been a foregone conclusion. Gary, as always, voted with Sara – for a quiet life. And Blue voted with his mum and dad, because that's what three-year-olds do.

Three against one. Outvoted, again. And Willow was sick of it! The soup – or what would be soup if the water ever boiled – slopped out of the pot and hissed into the fire as she stirred it angrily, round and round.

It had been another scorching, cloudless day – the latest in a long line of scorching, cloudless days. The drought was now official.

As they'd travelled down from the n~~~~
afternoon, the land had grown drier and ~~hat~~
They'd passed field after parched field, with ga~~~~
cracks and shrivelled crops. Dry river beds. Empt~~~~
ponds. In the towns, the fountains had been
switched off and the car-washes were closed "until
further notice". Hose-pipe bans were in force and
everyone was being encouraged to share a bath.

Willow, for her part, hadn't had a bath for weeks
– not since the last time they'd all paid her grandma
a visit, which was back in June. True, there had
been a stream at the last place they'd camped, and
Willow had swum in it every day. But it wasn't the
same as a tub full of hot water and bubbles. And
after seven hours inside the bus, that is what she
wanted more than anything in the world. A hot,
steaming, scented and oiled bath.

Willow looked round the gloomy clearing. Apart
from some hart's tongue fern and cuckoo pint,
there was nothing growing beneath the ancient oak.
It was too dark, too damp.

The cuckoo pint had already lost its purple rod
and twirl of fly-catching leaf, and a cluster of
orange berries gleamed from the top of the spike
instead. Willow sighed. She knew it would be up to
her to make sure that Blue didn't swallow any. Eight
years on the road, and her mum still had no idea
what was and what wasn't safe to eat.

She turned back to the soup. It had been on now

...r half an hour, yet the chopped vegetables ...re still raw and floating at the top of the pot, while the barley was scratchy at the bottom.

"Typical," Willow said irritably. "The whole country's tinder dry and Mum has to find the one place where the wood's damp."

She knelt down and blew into the smouldering logs. Clouds of smoke billowed up, sending the mosquitoes and midges flying off. She blew again, and again. The fire hissed and crackled. Suddenly, it burst into flames. Sparks and twists of flaming grass flew up into the overhanging branches.

Willow sat back on her heels and flicked a strand of hair, wet with sweat, out of her eyes. Despite the warmth of the evening and heat from the fire, she still felt shivery. The place had chilled her to the bones. Willow felt that she would never be warm again.

She crouched forwards over the fire, as close as she dared without scorching her sweatshirt, and stirred the soup. Round and round it went, as the liquid gradually came to the boil. Round and round and round. Diced carrots and potatoes, chopped onions and cabbage.

Willow stared unblinking into the steaming pot, mesmerized by the spinning circles of orange and white and green. It was like gazing down into the spinning vortex of a whirlwind or whirlpool. And as she stared, so Willow's eyes glazed over. She felt as if she was being pulled down into the central point of stillness. She felt dizzy. Her temples throbbed. All round her, she could hear voices. Hectoring. Yammering. Wailing...

And then someone screamed – someone outside Willow's head, not in. The vortex snapped shut. Willow dropped the spoon and leapt to her feet. "Blue!" she cried automatically.

But this time, it was not her little half-brother who had called out. He and Sara had been playing with a flock of sheep that Sara had fashioned from acorns and matchsticks. They were both looking as surprised as she was.

"Aaaghh!" the scream came again. High-pitched with terror, it didn't sound like Gary at all, yet it was coming from way up in the tree. "No, No, No," they heard him panting, breathless with fear.

"Gary!" Sara cried out, and ran towards the tree. Blue and Willow followed close behind her. All of them were looking up.

The next moment Gary himself appeared above their heads. He was shinning down the trunk as fast as he could. Twigs cracked, leaves fell. Finally, he swung himself down from a branch, tumbled through the air and landed awkwardly on his back. And there he lay – his eyes filled with fear – staring up into the tree.

Sara reached him first. She fell to the ground and went to cradle his head in her arms.

"Don't touch him!" Willow screamed.

Sara froze. "What? What?" she gasped.

"You should *never* move someone who's just had a bad fall," she said. "He could have broken his neck."

Gary twisted round slowly to one side. "I think I'm OK," he said. He pulled himself up on to his elbows. "Yeah, I'm fine." He smiled sheepishly. "Just a bit winded."

"But what *happened*?" said Sara. "Why did you scream?"

Gary climbed to his feet and dusted himself down. "Thought I saw something," he said. He sounded embarrassed.

"What?" said Willow, relieved to find that she might not be the only one to be spooked by their surroundings.

He paused and looked at her. "I don't know. I was just about to hammer the first nail in, like, when the air went all kind of – like when they blank out a face on the telly... You know, loads of little squares."

"Pixellated," said Willow.

"Yeah, that's right," said Gary slowly, his eyes narrowing as he struggled to remember exactly what he had seen. "Pixellated. Everything was shimmering. In this huge circle... No, more like a tunnel, it was. And I could hear these voices all round me, echoing, like they were coming out of the tunnel. Sad voices. Angry voices. Voices crying out in pain. And a smell. Disgusting, it was. Like burning flesh..." He paused and stared at Sara. "Do you think I'm going round the twist?" he said.

Sara laughed. "A bit too much sun, perhaps," she said.

"Well, *I* believe him," Willow broke in hotly. "I knew there was something horrible about this place."

"I believe him, too," said Sara, suddenly hushed and reverent. "This is a place of great energy," she said. "I felt it the moment we arrived."

"Did your crystals tingle?" Willow asked scornfully. She hated all the hippy-drippy nonsense her mum was always spouting.

Sara ignored her. "It is this energy, this power, this life force of the tree itself that we must harness," she said. Then she lifted her head, opened wide her arms, raised her palms and cried out to the tree. "You must help us to help you."

Willow cringed. For the first time since they'd arrived she was glad they had camped well away from the rest of the protesters. It might be dark and dank. It might be miles away from any water. It might even be haunted. But at least no one could see or hear her mum. Whenever Sara started ranting on in mystic mode, Willow just wanted to curl up and die.

"We apologize – spirit to spirit – for even *thinking*

of wounding your flesh," she announced. "We shall bind the platform in place instead. Then, together, we shall repel the destroyers. They will not clear this land. They will not rape this forest. No longer will they sacrifice trees at the altar of the internal combustion engine. The Bridgemorton bypass will never be built."

Then, apparently exhausted by her outburst, Sara let her arms go limp. Her head dropped. Willow rolled her eyes with impatience.

"I take it that means you want to stay here," she said.

Sara looked up slowly, and flicked her hair behind her ears. "Yes, Willow," she said. "I do. We have been guided to this place for a reason." She closed her eyes, breathed in and quivered. "There's something here. Something powerful. You can just *feel* it."

Willow shuddered. For once, she agreed with her mum. There *was* something there. But that was as far as their meeting of minds went. For whereas Sara Grant thought that the energy, or power, or life force – whatever – was benevolent, Willow was convinced that it was evil.

2

By the time they had finished supper, Gary was already saying that he had probably imagined the whole thing.

"I've never been that good with heights," he explained. "I go all giddy. Panicky. Remember that time Monty and I went up in the hot-air balloon?"

Willow nodded. She remembered it only too well. But that had been different. That time there had been a good reason for his being frightened.

"Good old Monty," he laughed. "We go back a long way. Why don't we see if he's here somewhere?"

Sara nodded enthusiastically. "Sure to be," she said. "You know what *he* thinks about roads. Come on," she said, jumping up. "We can do the dishes later."

"You mean *I* can," Willow muttered irritably under her breath. Somehow Sara was always busy doing something with Blue whenever the boring things had to be done. Still, if it meant getting away from this horrible oppressive place, she was all for it.

Five minutes later, they were ready to leave. Willow had packed her shoulder bag with all the things that she knew Sara would forget – a spare set of clothes for Blue, who still wasn't properly potty trained, a jar of citronella, a carton of juice and a torch for the walk back. Sara emerged from the bus wearing a long dress, a wide-brimmed straw hat and thong sandals. Blue was standing by the trunk of the oak tree in the middle of an imaginary game, giggling to himself and muttering some rhyme or other, over and over. Gary strode towards him.

"Gotcha!" he said, as he seized Blue round the middle and swung him up on to his shoulders. Blue giggled.

"Bye!" he cried, and waved back at the tree.

Gary looked round, but saw nothing. "All set?" he said.

"Yeah," came a chorus of assent, and off they went.

At first they kept to the bridleway. Although it was unused and overgrown, the bus had beaten a path through the encroaching branches and bracken, and they were able to walk three abreast. After a while, however, they heard voices and music to their left, and cut up through the woods in single file.

Sara went first, picking her way daintily through the undergrowth. Gary followed close behind. He was stooping low, so that Blue wouldn't bang his head on the overhanging trees. It meant he couldn't see where he was going. Time and again, thorny branches and brambles snagged on his clothes, before flicking back behind him. Willow, who was bringing up the rear, had to keep her distance.

Once upon a time it had all been so very different. She remembered how Roy – her own dad – used to carry her on his shoulders, with Sara walking by their side. They were a family. A unit. But then Roy had left...

Willow looked ahead sadly. She watched her mum, her mum's partner and her mum and partner's child as they bobbed away in front of her. Tears welled up in her eyes.

When Gary had first appeared on the scene, her mum had tried her best to ensure that Willow never felt excluded. But the birth of Blue, three years later, had changed all that. Sara suddenly had a new family, and Willow found herself being side-lined – or that was how it seemed. She felt like an interloper. An outsider. Three weeks earlier, Willow had turned seventeen. Perhaps the time had now come for her to set out on her own. "After all," she thought miserably, "no one'll miss me."

"Are you all right, back there?" Gary called.

Willow looked up, suddenly guilty for feeling so sorry for herself. She wiped her eyes on her sleeve. "Fine," she said.

"We're nearly there!" Blue announced. "I can see camp-fires. Come on, Wills."

Willow smiled to herself. How could she even think of leaving? After all, who would look after Blue if she was gone? Who would remember to bring a change of clothes, or stop him from eating poisonous berries? He, at least, still needed her. Of course they were still a family – a little unconventional perhaps, but no more so than many others.

"Hurry up, then," said Gary. He was standing waiting for her, a taut branch of elder clasped in his hand. Willow ran to catch up and slipped through the gap. The elder slapped back into place like a door slamming shut on the depths of the forest.

Willow sighed. "At last," she murmured.

"Beautiful, eh?" said Gary. He put Blue down on the ground and gazed round the rolling woodland. "And they want to cut all this down so the good people of Bridgemorton can have their blasted bypass."

Willow nodded. It was truly lovely, enchanting – like something out of a fairy-tale. Certainly far too lovely to be turned into yet another service station. While Gary walked on, she stood for a moment taking it all in, horribly aware that if their protest came to nothing, there might never be another chance.

There were beech trees and ash trees, and silver birches with their peeling white slivers of papery bark, all casting long shadows in the golden birdsung twilight. And where the sunlight struck the forest floor, woodland flowers glistened like jewels – pink, purple, gleaming yellow-white. There were clusters of toadstools: ink caps, puffballs, crimson fly agaric – more dangers to warn Blue about. There were rooks' nests and blackbirds' nests. Rabbit warrens. Owl pellets. Nestlings and seedlings and fallen tree trunks, spongy with decay.

The whole cycle, thought Willow. Life, death and rebirth...

"Pooh!" said Blue. Willow looked down, her moment of understanding broken. She couldn't help smiling at his face, all screwed up with exaggerated disgust. "What's that horrid smell?" he wanted to know.

"Smell?" said Willow. "I can't..." She sniffed the air and looked round. There *was* something. Something metallic, juicy, faintly pungent.

She soon spotted where it came from. Growing at the base of the elderberry bush was some wild garlic. It was past its best. The spiked leaves were duller than they had once been, and most of the flowers had already gone to seed. It was unusual for it to smell at this time of year. Perhaps she'd crushed some underfoot.

Willow stepped back. Odd, she thought, as she looked from left to right. Usually wild garlic grew in clumps. Here, on the other hand, it was strung out in a long curving line which hugged the edge of the deepest forest. She frowned, puzzled.

"Wil–low!" Blue complained, his fingers clamped over his nose. "What is that sbell?"

Willow looked down at him and smiled. "Ramsons," she said. "Wild garlic."

Blue unclamped his nose, and a broad grin spread over his face. "Garlic?" he said, and giggled.

"Yeah, garlic," said Willow. "What's so funny?"

But Blue didn't answer. Instead, he turned on his heels and stomped off over the forest floor, chanting to the fall of his marching feet. "Ring of garlic! Garlic ring! It keeps the evil out! It keeps the evil in! Ring of garlic! Garlic ring..."

Willow stared after him. Where had this new rhyme come from? Certainly she hadn't taught it to him. And why *was* the garlic growing so curiously? It was too much of a coincidence. Her heart beat furiously. A tremor of apprehension quivered down her spine. Had Blue experienced something strange at the tree too?

"Blue!" she cried out. "What are you saying? What does it mean?"

"It keeps the evil out! It keeps the evil in!" Blue called back.

Willow raced after him, crouched down in front of him and seized him by the wrists. "Listen to me, Blue," she said, trying hard to remain calm. "This new nursery rhyme. Where did you learn it?"

Blue put his finger over his lips and began to whisper. "Ring of garlic! Garlic ring! It—"

"Stop being so infuriating, and tell me!" Willow shouted. She shook him. "Tell me where you heard it!"

"I can't," said Blue, tears welling up in his eyes.

"Why not?" Willow demanded.

"Because ... because I promised," he sobbed.

"And who did you promise?" she said, horrified to discover how easy it was for her to sound exactly like her mum.

Blue clamped his lips firmly together. He wasn't that stupid! He wiped his eyes, and stared back at her defiantly.

"Who?" Willow said. "Who? Who?" her voice getting louder and louder. "*Who?*"

Blue was shocked. The colour drained from his face. His body trembled. He had never seen his sister so angry before. The glaring eyes were frightening him. His mouth opened a fraction.

"The two naughty boys," he said.

Willow breathed in noisily. She remembered the game she'd seen him playing by the oak tree before they'd left. The same icy fingers began strumming up and down her spine. "Was that who you said goodbye to?" she said. "Were they up in the tree?"

"Yes!" Blue howled, and burst into tears. "And they told me not to tell anyone. And now I have. And now they'll get me, like they said. And it's all your fault!"

"Oh, Blue," said Willow gently, and wrapped her arms around him. "No one's going to get you. I wouldn't let them."

But Blue was inconsolable. "They will," he insisted. "They will!" And he began howling all the louder.

"What on earth's going on back there?" called Gary.

Willow looked up. Gary and Sara were standing, hand in hand, about a hundred metres further on.

"It's all right," she called back. "We're just coming."

Sara turned and disappeared over the ridge. Gary waited for them to catch up. As they approached him, Willow spoke hurriedly to Blue. She didn't want him telling anyone about the "naughty boys". Not yet, at any rate.

"I'm sorry," she said. "I really am. And I didn't mean to frighten you. I ... I just had to know. That's all."

Blue nodded sullenly. "Carry," he said.

Willow bent down, picked him up and continued

without breaking her stride. She whispered into his ear.

"I don't think the two naughty boys will mind you telling me, because I'm your sister. But anybody else..." She paused dramatically.

Willow knew her mum. If Sara thought the tree might be haunted by some kind of spirit, she would be out with the Ouija board before you could say prestidigitation. And that was something Willow wanted to prevent at all costs. If there *was* something evil about the tree, the last thing they wanted to do was invite it in.

"I won't tell anyone else," said Blue.

"Good boy," said Willow, and she kissed him on the top of his head.

3

As Willow and Blue reached the top of the slope, the woodland opened up before them.

"Wow!" Blue gasped, his recent tears instantly forgotten. He wriggled in Willow's arms to be put down.

Willow raised her eyebrows in surprise. "I didn't realize there'd be so many people," she said.

Gary nodded. "There's a lot of bad feeling about this particular bypass," he said. "People are angry that the proposal to dig a tunnel through the hill has been shelved. Of course it wouldn't be perfect, but it'd be a damned sight better than the road coming right through the forest."

"So why don't they?" said Willow.

Gary's eyes narrowed. He rubbed his finger and

thumb together. "Money," he said. "As always." He turned away in disgust.

Sara had already spotted someone she knew and was laughing and chatting down by a huge bonfire on the edge of the encampment. Blue ran down the hill towards her. Willow and Gary followed him.

The camp was huge. There must have been forty vehicles of all shapes and sizes parked up: converted buses like their own, beat-up Landrovers with trailers and caravans, pick-up trucks and vans – all nestling under the trees. Dotted about between them were campfires and tents, benders draped in plastic sheeting – and people. Lots of people.

Willow's heart swelled with pride. There they were, men, women and children who had come from all over the country to protest about the destruction of yet another piece of countryside. Men, women and children who cared.

Willow had gone to school for eighteen months in a twee little town called Mabelfield. She'd been stuck in a class with snotty, mindless kids who laughed at her clothes and her accent, whose fathers were dentists, lawyers, bankers, and whose mothers did a lot of work for charity. They drove round in Range Rovers and BMWs.

She remembered one lesson where Mrs Arneson was banging on about global warming. Apart from Willow herself, none of the class was interested. Louisa Padgett had actually fallen asleep. Later,

Willow had heard her talking to some of the other girls.

"It was just so *booo-ring*," she said. "Anyway, Daddy's just had a catalytic converter put in the Merc, so *we're* all right."

Even now, the girl's words made Willow prickle with indignation. On the other hand, she thought, it was about time Gary sorted out the exhaust on the bus. Every time he revved up, clouds of dark grey billowed up, blocking the view behind.

She looked over at Gary. The last rays of sunshine were glinting on his cropped hair, his wispy beard, the tip of his determined nose. Sensing her looking at him, he turned and smiled. His teeth flashed and his blue eyes crinkled and gleamed. Willow smiled back. It was not the time to mention the state of the bus. Gary was a good person. He didn't want to foul up the air wherever he drove, but the quote he'd received for an overhaul of the engine had been for almost five hundred pounds – five hundred pounds he didn't have. Once again, it all came down to money.

"Look who's here," Sara announced as Gary and Willow approached.

"Hiya, Ally!" said Gary.

"Hello, Gary!" said Ally. "Welcome to Camp Didgeridoo." She turned to Willow. "Hi, my name's... My God!" she exclaimed. "Willow, it's you! Haven't you grown! Oh, forgive me," she said, and kissed Willow on both cheeks. "I swore I would never say that. But, Jeez you were just a kid..."

"I've just hit seventeen," said Willow. It was good meeting Ally again. She and Sara were old friends, and seeing them together again took her back to the time when Roy had still been around.

"It must be five ... six years since I last saw you," Ally was saying. "Do you remember? We rented that cottage below the cliff. You, me, Sara, Roy and what's his face?"

"Damien," Willow reminded her, and giggled.

Ally had had loads of boyfriends back then, but Damien was without doubt the worst. He was scrawny, whiney, tight-fisted and had breath so bad it could stun you at five paces.

"Damien," Ally repeated dreamily. "I wonder where he ended up."

"He got a job with a gas company," said Sara.

"Figures!" said Ally, and burst out laughing. "Pffworr! Talk about natural gas."

"There was nothing natural about Damien's breath," Sara spluttered, and the pair of them started laughing all over again.

"And what about Roy?" said Ally finally. "What's he up to? Last thing I heard, he was out in Madagascar."

Willow looked away, disappointed. She'd been hoping that Ally might have more recent news of her dad. Madagascar had been three years earlier.

Since then, he'd been to Armenia, Honduras and Mali.

"Oh, off doing his bit," Sara said somewhat dismissively.

"Well, I think what he does is great," Willow said. Her dad worked for CrisisAid, a relief operation that delivered essential food, clothing and equipment to people who needed it. Sara disapproved. "It's like using a sticking plaster to cure cancer," was her favourite expression. This evening, however, Sara seemed unwilling to talk about Roy – even negatively.

"So who's here?" she said, glancing round.

"Oh, everyone," said Ally, relieved to fill the awkward silence. "Curly. Mole. Tag and Jules. Oh, and Marnie, Pete and the boys. Dexter. Tom. Fliss. The Chate twins – who are talking to one another for a change. Crimper. Sleaze. Steg. Tashie—"

"Have you seen Monty?" Gary interrupted.

"Yeah," said Ally, nodding her head vigorously. "He's here. He's staying down the track a bit in a separate camp." She laughed, "Crow's Nest Camp, it's called. They're all camping up the top of the trees. Got platforms and rope-ladders, and these walkways strung out between the trees. Some of them have been up there for weeks."

Gary smiled. "Nothing wrong with Monty's head for heights, then," he said, and he shivered as his own terror at being high up in the oak tree flashed before him.

"Actually, I saw him this morning," Ally was saying. "He said he might be up here this evening. I—" She stopped abruptly, and her face broke into a grin. "Talk of the devil," she said. "Monty! Monty!" she called. "Over here."

Willow looked round. Standing at the front of the queue for what the sign described as *Mulled Punch* was a tall man, dressed in a tweed jacket and grey flannels. His hair looked a bit thinner than before, but otherwise Thomas (Monty) Montague-Smithers hadn't changed a bit.

"Gary, Ally, Willow," he beamed. "Good to see you all. But where's..." At that moment Blue emerged from behind Sara's skirt. "*There* he is!" said Monty. "Baby Blue – except you're not a baby any more, are you?"

"No, I'm not," said Blue crossly.

Monty chuckled and turned back to the woman behind the counter. "Make that five, Lucy," he said. "And an orange juice, please."

Willow smiled to herself. Monty was one of those people who had the knack of enthusing others. No one could resist that big lop-sided grin of his.

"Here we go, then," he said, as he handed round the drinks. "Let's go and sit over by one of the fires. Catch up on the news," he laughed, and clapped his hand on Gary's shoulder. "Like what happened to your hair."

Gary groaned. "Head lice, mate," he said. "I couldn't stand the itching."

Monty pulled himself away theatrically. "Ugh!" he cried.

"It's all right now," Gary laughed. He rubbed his hand over his head. "Sara found these old electric clippers in an Oxfam shop. I rig them up to the battery once every few weeks for Blue and me. No hair. No lice. No worries."

"I never get them myself," Sara added casually. "Nor does Willow."

Willow scowled. The only reason *she* never got them was because she went through her hair with a fine-toothed comb three times a day – something neither Gary nor Blue could be bothered to do. As for her mum, Willow suspected Sara washed her hair in the chemical shampoos she refused to let the others use, whenever no one was watching.

Monty ran his fingers through his own thinning hair. "So, Gary," he said. "What have you been doing since Reagley? My God, that was a fiasco," he said and, without waiting for Gary to answer his question, he was off.

Willow settled herself down with her cup of mulled punch. She couldn't remember the number of times, when she was younger, that Monty had held her spellbound with his stories – even those she had heard before. As he got into the tale of the ill-fated hot-air balloon escapade, Willow was relieved to find that he hadn't lost his touch. He stood up to act out better the difficulty they'd had inflating the balloon. He did the voices of all those involved. He interspersed the tale with jokes and asides.

"So there we were," he said, "Sara, Gary and myself, rising up in this overgrown shopping basket, with a light westerly breeze taking us precisely where we wanted to go: the Reagley Manor Hunt."

"We should never have gone up in the first place," Sara said, shaking her head. Everyone shooshed her. "Well!" she complained.

"The plan," Monty continued, "was fiendishly simple. We had klaxons to frighten the horses, a sackful of pungent herbs and spices to put the dogs off the scent, and reams of anti-hunt leaflets to annoy the red-jacketed ones." He turned and looked round at his audience, one after the other. His eyes twinkled. "Never for a moment did we imagine just how annoyed they would become."

Willow laughed. She remembered how she and Blue had followed the balloon across a field, until they'd come to the other saboteurs and protesters who were standing by the gates of the manor house. As the balloon had got nearer – klaxons blazing, paper and pungent powder tumbling down through the air, the sign on the side proclaiming "An End to ALL Blood Sports" – all those taking part in the hunt had gone wild.

"Frothing at the mouth, they were, and baying for blood," said Monty. He laughed. "And the animals were worse! The dogs howled and snapped at anything that came too close to them. The horses whinnied and reared up. One portly old trout got deposited in a water trough. Another landed in a heap of manure." He laughed again. "And then I spotted this old chap standing apart from the rest."

Again, he paused for effect. Again, his audience moved in that little bit closer – except for Blue who, despite himself, had drifted off to sleep in Sara's lap.

"He had a face the colour of a good Burgundy," said Monty softly, "and a silver handlebar moustache. He slipped his monocle into his top pocket, raised his shotgun to his eye, took aim, and fired. Bang! Bang!"

Willow closed her eyes. She could still picture it all so well: the bullets hitting the balloon (even Colonel Blimp couldn't have missed so large a sitting target) and emerging at the other side. Two large flapping holes marking where they had passed through. And she remembered something else – something she felt uneasy about, even now.

It was Mrs Arneson who had introduced her to the Balloon Game. The poor woman had played it in an attempt to motivate her pupils. The rules were simple.

Ten volunteers were selected to fly in a hot-air balloon. Each one was given the name of the famous person they were to role-play. Then they were told the balloon was about to crash. The only way for anyone to survive was if others were thrown overboard to lighten the load. To qualify for a continued place in the balloon, each person had to give a one-minute talk explaining why he or she should not be chucked out. At the end of each round, there was a vote.

The final result at Mabelfield County School had been no great surprise to Willow. Among others, J.F.K., Albert Schweitzer, Marie Curie, Martin Luther King and Mother Theresa were all swiftly dispatched. Sean Rafferty (American TV hunk) and Angelina Priori (catwalk sex-bomb) were not. Angelina won on a re-count.

As Willow had stared up at the crippled hot-air balloon, she had found herself playing that same game. Naturally, the first choice was easy. Monty would have to go, even if he was the only one up there who knew what he was doing.

But who then? Gary or Sara? Sara? Or Gary?

Of course she knew who she ought to choose – who everyone would *expect* her to choose. Sara was her mum, for heaven's sake! Her own flesh and blood. How could she even consider choosing anyone else? And yet she had.

After all, she'd reasoned, Gary would look after

her and Blue if Sara wasn't around. She knew he would. Whereas Sara would fall apart if she found herself on her own again. It had been bad enough when Roy had left. If Gary went too, she'd go to pieces. She wouldn't be able to cope.

And so Willow had chosen Gary to survive, while her mum she was prepared to see tossed overboard. In the end, of course, they had all made it down safely, yet the choice she had made remained something which gnawed at her guiltily, something which Willow would never be able to forget.

She opened her eyes and looked round. Gary was poking at the fire. Sara was laughing. Blue muttered in his sleep and rolled over. They looked so beautiful in the flickering firelight. She loved them all.

How could I ever choose between any of them? she wondered and shivered. *God knows, I hope I never really have to.*

4

All too soon, the evening of reunions, recollections and regaling with stories came to an end. It was time for Sara, Gary, Blue and Willow to head back to their own isolated campsite. Ally tried to persuade them to spend the night with her up at Camp Didgeridoo, but Sara was adamant.

"I want to wake up in the place we found," she said. "It's so peaceful and secluded."

Willow sighed unhappily. Too peaceful, she thought, and far too secluded. If anything happened to them, it would be ages before they were discovered. Pushing such gruesome thoughts aside, she climbed to her feet and pulled her torch from her bag. Sara kissed everyone goodbye, Gary picked up Blue, and the four of them set off back up the wooded slope.

As the glow from the fires receded, and the babble of talking voices, laughter and music faded away, Willow felt her heart begin to race. There was no moon, and the stars, though bright in the sky, cast no light below. Willow shone her torch this way and that, pointing it nervously at every suspicious shadow, into every corner of ominous darkness.

"Stop darting about with the light," Sara complained irritably.

"Sorry," said Willow. She hadn't spotted anything untoward, yet her misgivings persisted. To please her mum, however, she kept the beam of light pointing directly ahead. Across the forest floor, up the flower-speckled banks of grass, bouncing off the trees and off towards the deeper, darker part of the forest where even the sun found it hard to break through.

They continued in silence. Sara was at the front, Willow behind her, with Gary and the sleeping Blue bringing up the rear. Abruptly, Sara disappeared into a dense patch of bushy undergrowth. All round her, Willow smelt a familiar juicy yet metallic odour. She knew she was crossing the garlic once again – the ring of garlic.

Behind her, she heard Blue muttering in his sleep. Gary, for whom the words meant nothing, did not notice what his little son was saying.

Willow, on the other hand, could not help but notice.

"*It keeps the evil out!*" he whispered. "*It keeps the evil in!*"

The same words. The same awful words.

Like everyone else, Willow knew that a ring of garlic – proper garlic – was supposed to keep vampires, hobgoblins and ghouls at bay. An unbroken chain would not allow any evil to pass through. But what if the rhyme was right? What if the ring of garlic could enclose the evil, locking it up within its embrace?

Willow gasped. The four of them were now inside that circle themselves. She began shuddering all over again, and her sense of unease grew as she stumbled and tripped down the narrow forest path. Branches slapped her face, briars and brambles scratched her arms and legs. Overhead, the forest canopy closed, shutting out even the starlight.

"Here's the bridleway," Sara announced.

"Turn right," said Gary. "The bus should be about a hundred metres further on."

The thought of arriving back at their campsite did nothing to alleviate Willow's fears. It was all she could do to make her wobbly legs keep walking. After all, with every step they took, they were getting closer to the centre of the evil circle: the ancient oak tree.

By the time they reached the clearing, Willow

was shivering uncontrollably. Her teeth chattered. Her body shook. After the warm and friendly atmosphere of Camp Didgeridoo, their own campsite seemed all the more awful. Cold. Damp. Menacing. She looked at the tent where she and Blue normally slept. Small and horribly flimsy, it would offer no protection against whatever was out there.

"I think Blue should sleep in the bus with us," Sara announced as she lit one of the lamps and a swarm of insects instantly glued themselves to the glass. "I'm too tired to check the tent for mosquitoes."

"Will the bus be any better?" asked Gary.

Sara nodded. "I lit a coil before we left. It should have done the trick."

Willow smiled at her mum's hypocrisy. Sara was always going on about the pesticides and fungicides and weed-killers that farmers sprayed on their fields, yet when it came to mozzies, she herself had never held back. Apart from the citronella, she used fly-sprays, chemical creams, electric zappers – anything to avoid being bitten. In Willow's opinion, the snake-like green coils were the worst. They burned slowly from the outside, round and round to the centre, emitting a sweet toxic smoke as they smouldered. The smell made her feel sick.

Tonight, however, Willow was prepared to put up with the acrid smoke, the itchy eyes, the runny nose, not to mention Gary's snoring or her mum's incessant sleep-talking. She would have put up with anything at all rather than spend the night on her own, outside, beneath the creepy oak tree.

She followed the others up the steps of the bus. "I think I'll join you tonight," she said as casually as she could manage. "I don't fancy being bitten either."

She didn't mention that wild horses wouldn't drag her back outside.

Despite her concerns, despite her fears, despite the growing sense of foreboding which had gripped her since she had crossed back over that circle of garlic, the moment Willow crawled into her sleeping bag, she fell into a deep and dreamless sleep.

Outside the moon rose, gibbous and bright, though little of its light penetrated beneath the dense cover of oak leaves. A thin mist coiled its way out of the ground and swirled around the gnarled roots of the tree, encircled the trunk and crept slowly higher and higher. An owl swooped down on quilted wings, talons outstretched. A moment later the stillness was shattered by the screech of some unfortunate rodent. And then the silence descended again, thick and suffocating, like a dusty shroud.

The hours passed, and Willow emerged from the empty depths of her sleep. Her eyelids flickered as pictures flitted before her – as vivid as a succession of film clips.

She was stirring the soup again. Round and round it went, thud, thud, thud!

Thud?

Willow looked down. An onion, unskinned and unchopped, had somehow found its way into the pot. It was banging against the side as she stirred.

Willow turned the onion over in her hand. The hot skin steamed. She placed it on the chopping board, raised the knife and chopped it in two. The two halves fell on their sides, the rings oozing and glinting in the fire glow.

There was a rustle in the bushes. Willow looked up. There it was again. She stood up silently, tiptoed across the clearing and crouched down beneath the branches of a dense elderberry bush. The rustle came again, human, furtive – and getting nearer.

Got to get out of here, she thought. *Got to escape.*

There was the sound of metal grinding on metal, and a click, followed by a whiff of gunpowder. A twig cracked immediately to her right. She should have stayed put, she should have remained under cover – but that was not the scenario the dream had planned for her.

Running. Running. As fast as her legs would carry her, she raced through the undergrowth, back to the safety of the fire. She grasped the chopping knife, and crouched down behind the bubbling pot, panting with fear and expectation.

The footsteps continued. Nearer and nearer they came. All at once, there was a gasp. The footsteps halted.

Silence.

Heart pumping, temples thumping, Willow peered round the side of the pot. There was something there. Something monstrous. It stared at her from between the leafy branches. Bulging eyes. Blood-red bloated features. Swollen tongue.

Willow screamed and looked away. Her gaze fell on the onion halves. They were still glistening, but no longer with the milky onion juice. Blood, deep and dark, was now oozing from between the rings.

The whole atmosphere throbbed with unhappiness. Willow felt herself overcome with a feeling of grief. Her throat ached with sadness and tears welled up in her eyes. Before she knew it she was crying, sobbing, choking with streaming tears.

"Willow!" a voice called.

Willow turned away, and clamped her hands over her ears. "Leave me alone," she whimpered.

But the voice called again, loud and insistent. "Willow! Will-*ow*! Willow, wake up!"

Willow sat bolt upright. She stared round her wildly, unable for a second to make sense of her surroundings. She rubbed her eyes. Slowly, gradually, things slipped back into their familiar place.

She was in the bus, cocooned in her sleeping bag and dripping with sweat. In front of her was a face – her mum's face. Her lips were quivering, her eyes were wet with tears.

"Willow," she said, "you've got to get up and help us. It's Blue..."

"What?" Willow demanded, suddenly alert and afraid. "What's happened to him?"

Sara sniffed and wiped her eyes, "I don't know," she said. "He's not here. He's disappeared."

5

Willow immediately jumped out of her sleeping bag and got herself dressed. *Not Blue, not Blue, not Blue!* She repeated the same two words over and over in her head as she pulled on her jeans, her T-shirt, her socks and shoes. Please don't let anything have happened to Blue.

She raced outside. It was half-past six. Unlike her, the sun had already been up for hours, yet the clearing beneath the spreading oak tree was still bathed in dark shadows. There was no birdsong. The air smelt of decay.

Gary was off in the woods some way to her right. She could hear him calling Blue's name. "Blu-ue! Blu-ue!" He sounded calm still, confident that at any moment Blue would reply and come running.

Sara, on the other hand, was dashing about the clearing like a headless chicken.

"Blue!" she screamed desperately into the dark forest. "Where are you, my angel? *BLUE!*" She turned and saw Willow standing by the bus. "Oh Willow," she gasped, "what could have happened to him? He's so young. He's so *trusting*!"

"Don't worry," said Willow, trying hard to still her own frantically hammering heart.

"But where is he?" said Sara. "Where *is* he?"

Willow sighed. Her mum was not a person to miss the opportunity of turning a problem into a crisis. "He'll be fine," she said. "He's probably just wandered off a bit too far. If he doesn't turn up by seven, I'll go up to Camp Didgeridoo and get some volunteers to help look for him, OK? In the meantime, I think both of us should check along the bridleway."

Sara nodded her head jerkily. "Seven o'clock," she said. "All right." She smiled weakly. "Sometimes I don't know what I'd do without you," she said.

Willow looked away. It made her feel strangely resentful when Sara talked to her like that. She wanted her mum to look after her, to take care of her – not depend on her. What with her and Blue, instead of feeling like a daughter and a sister, most of the time Willow felt like a mother of two.

"Any sign of him back there?" Gary called out from the trees.

"Not yet," Sara called back. "We're just about to check the bridleway."

"Good idea," said Gary. "Blu-ue!" he called. "Blu-ue!"

At the bridleway, Sara and Willow split up. Sara returned the way the bus had come the day before, while Willow opted to go deeper into the forest. The track soon grew both narrower and more difficult to navigate as the undergrowth encroached from both sides. It was like making her way along a long, dark tunnel, full of treacherous obstacles.

"Blue!" she shouted. There was no echo. Her voice, though urgent, sounded curiously dead — like someone shouting in a soundproofed room. She stumbled further on, carefully pushing the thorned branches aside, jumping over fallen trees and wading through dense patches of bracken and stinging nettles. "Blue! Can you hear me, Blue?"

She fell still, paused, and cocked her head to one side. Perhaps he hadn't wandered off at all. Perhaps he was close by, but unable to reply. She listened intently. He could have fallen down a hole. Or waded out of his depth into a marsh. Or what if he'd got caught in a trap set for some animal? Anything might have happened.

And then she heard it — faint at first, but

unmistakable – the sound of giggling, and it was coming from where she'd started out.

"You fool!" she groaned. "The tree!"

Spinning on her heels, she raced back along the track. The giggling grew louder, mocking, chiding. The nettles stung her hands, the brambles scratched her legs. Once she tripped. Once she cracked her shin painfully on a tree stump. But she didn't ease up for a moment.

The clearing was deserted and eerily quiet. Willow stopped, caught her breath and looked round. Sara and Gary were nowhere to be seen – or heard. And, Willow reasoned, if she couldn't hear them shouting out Blue's name, then neither would they be able to hear her.

Chewing nervously on the inside of her mouth, Willow started walking towards the tree. She had the feeling that someone – or something – was watching her. Once again, she was shuddering. And despite her pumping heart and sweating brow, she felt chilled to the bone.

If this was a film, ominous, discordant music would be playing and Willow knew she would be sitting on the edge of her seat, willing the character on screen to turn back. But it wasn't a film, and Willow had to go on.

"Blue?" she whispered uncertainly, and stared at the tree. "Are you there, Blue?"

The feeling of being watched persisted. She

stepped over the flock of abandoned acorn-sheep and their lollipop-stick pen, and peered up into the branches.

Sara was certainly right about the tree – it *was* magnificent. Towering high above Willow, it must have been at least forty metres tall – and as for the girth of the trunk, she wouldn't even like to guess how wide it was. The thick green foliage trembled and hissed in a gathering breeze.

Willow trembled with a growing sense of impending doom. Something was about to happen, she just knew it was.

Suddenly the sound of giggling erupted from high above her head. Willow's eyes narrowed.

"Blue!" she screamed. "Is that you?"

There was no reply, but Willow thought she heard the sound of furtive rustling.

As she continued to comb the branches for any sight of the boy, so the dense cover of green leaves began to telescope in and out before her eyes. She felt dizzy. She felt sick. The gleaming green leaves began to flash and break up, just as Gary had described. Willow was appalled. It was happening again.

All at once, the face from her nightmare came back, floating above her in all its bulging, blood-red, bloated horror. Could *that* be Blue? she wondered miserably. Could the dream have been some awful premonition? But even as she thought it, so the face disappeared, and with it the air of overwhelming sadness.

In its place came angry voices, stuttering with fury. Then other voices, pleading, tearful. Then chanting ... then screaming ... then jeering ... And as Willow stood there, with the bewildering sequence of sounds echoing all round her, so faces and objects also emerged and faded in the pixellated green blur.

A brutish, swarthy face. A knotted rope. A wild-eyed horse. Dripping blood. Musket fire and arrow twang. A man dressed in black robes, his head concealed inside a tall, pointed hood. A hideous woman with a face cobble-stoned with warts... And then the giggling again, and a flash of three grimy faces grinning down at her.

One of the faces was familiar. "Blue!" she said and, as she spoke, the ever-changing images came to an abrupt halt.

Her brother – for it was definitely him – was standing up on a horizontal branch waving down at her. The branch was broad, but far too high up for a three-year-old who wasn't holding on. Willow felt her chest tighten. She wanted him down, but in one piece.

"Just crouch down," she said gently, "and hold on to that thin branch by your foot."

Blue did as he was told. Instantly the two boys, who were standing on either side of him, began jeering.

"Scaredy-cat! Scaredy-cat! Don't know what you're looking at!"

Blue immediately sprang back upright. "I'm not scared," he said defiantly.

Willow's heart missed a beat. "Blue!" she said. "Be careful!"

"Blue, be careful!" the two boys taunted.

Willow felt herself growing angry. "I mean it!" she said.

"I mean it!" the two boys repeated, in their mocking sing-song voice, and all three burst out giggling.

Willow didn't know what to do. Normally, Blue was such a good boy – he would do anything for her. But not now. He was clearly in thrall to the two older boys, who looked about seven or eight, and was desperately trying not to lose face.

"Please climb down," said Willow. "I'd hate you to slip and hurt yourself."

The two boys put their arms around Blue and whispered into his ears. Blue smiled. They whispered again. Blue nodded, spread his arms wide apart and began flapping wildly.

"Blue!" Willow said sharply. But Blue was no longer listening to her. He moved forward until his toes were sticking over the edge of the branch, and leant into the wind. Willow gasped.

"Now," whispered the two boys.

"*No!*" Willow screamed. But it was already too

late. With his arms still flapping, Blue launched himself off the branch.

A loud whooshing sound filled the air, and the voices and faces came fast and furious, one after the other, in rewind gibberish. The shimmering green circle opened up into a long, spinning tunnel. And in the middle of it all was Blue, wide-eyed and arched back, tumbling out of the tree.

"Wheeeee!" he squealed as he hurtled down to the ground.

Willow dashed about, this way and that, arms reaching upwards. She knew if he struck the ground, he would break his neck. Down, down, down he fell – he was going to miss her! She staggered backwards and...

CRASH!

Blue thumped down into Willow's chest, and the pair of them ended up sprawling on the ground. Blue giggled, and Willow – who was too relieved to be angry – hugged him tightly and kissed him again and again.

"Yuck!" Blue announced, and pushed her away. "Stop that soppy stuff at once."

Willow released her hold sadly. She'd known, of course, that one day Blue would object to kisses and cuddles – she'd just hoped it wouldn't be so soon. She watched him climb to his feet and look up into the tree.

"Who's up there?" she asked.

"No one," said Blue. "They've gone again."

"The two naughty boys?" said Willow. She shivered with unease.

Blue nodded. "Eddy and Jack," he said. "They're my friends." And then he added, "They can fly."

Willow looked at his earnest little face. How could she explain to him about the boys when she herself didn't understand what they were? Ghosts? Spirits? Hobgoblins? They had looked so *real*. One thing was for sure, even if they could fly, Blue certainly couldn't. Willow crouched down beside him and held him by the wrists.

"I want you to promise me," she said, "that you will never *ever* jump off somewhere so high again."

Blue looked away. Maybe he was frightened that she was going to get angry again. Maybe he just felt he was too old now to be told what to do. Whatever, he didn't reply.

"Promise me," Willow repeated.

"OK, I promise," said Blue sullenly. "Now leave me alone."

Willow could feel her anger rising again. "No," she said. "There's something else. I still don't want you to say anything to Mum or Dad about the two boys. OK?"

Blue looked bored.

"OK?" she said again.

"All *right*!" he said wearily. He pulled his arms free, sank them deep into his dungarees' pockets and slouched off back to the bus, pausing only to kick at the flock of acorn sheep. Willow sighed. For a three-year-old, Blue was doing a pretty good impersonation of a stroppy teenager.

As the door of the bus slammed shut, Sara came back from her search along the bridleway. She looked at Willow, she looked at the bus – and frowned.

"Who was that?" she said.

"It was Blue," Willow said. "I just found him." She laughed. "But I don't think he wanted to be found."

Sara shook her head in disbelief. "But why didn't he answer when we called for him?" she said. "That's not like him."

Willow shrugged. It was something that had been bothering her, too. Often, when he was engrossed in a game, he would fail to hear his name being called – but never for so long. Either he had deliberately ignored them or... But no, it was a stupid idea – an impossible idea.

"Oh, well," said Sara, "never mind. I'm just happy he's back. I thought I'd take him into Bridgemorton for a look round. Do you fancy coming?"

"No," said Willow vaguely. "No, thanks. I was thinking I'd go back up to Camp Didgeridoo—"

"Whatever," Sara interrupted. She turned to the bus. "Blue?" she called.

The door opened and Blue emerged. He was looking decidedly shamefaced. "I'm sorry," he said at once.

"Come and give me a hug," said Sara.

Blue trotted down the steps and across the clearing to an open-armed Sara. "I didn't mean to," he blurted out. "I trod on them by accident." He pointed back to the pile of sheep, some without heads, some without legs.

Sara laughed. "Is *that* why you didn't answer me?" she said. "Oh, Blue, angel! Mummy wouldn't have been cross."

Willow smiled to herself. Good old Blue! With one brilliant misunderstanding he had ruled out all of Sara's questions about where he had been and what he had been doing. As far as she was concerned, he'd been hiding – that was all.

As Willow watched them disappear into the woods, hand in hand, her smile faded. Whatever her mum now believed, Willow knew that Blue had not deliberately hidden himself at all. He'd been up in the oak tree playing with two boys who didn't exist!

"Blu-ue!" she heard. "Blu-ue!"

It was Gary returning, still calling out in the same calm and patient way. Willow cupped her hands to her mouth.

"It's OK, Gary," she bellowed. "We've found him."

The next moment, Gary appeared. There were beads of sweat on his forehead and his vest was soaked through.

"Where is he now?" he asked.

"Mum's taken him into town," said Willow.

Gary nodded. "And where had he been all that time?"

"Up the tree," said Willow, and rolled her eyes.

Gary stared at her as if she was mad. "Up the tree?" he repeated. "He couldn't get up there. He's far too small."

"But..." Willow began. She turned and looked back at the imposing oak tree – and started with surprise. Was she losing her mind? She ran over to the trunk and stood in the dusty footprints she had made earlier. She looked up.

"No!" she murmured, and her whole body shuddered with foreboding.

The branch – the big, broad, horizontal branch, the branch that the three boys had been standing on, the branch that Blue had launched himself from – it wasn't there. An ugly blackened scar in the trunk of the tree marked where it would have been attached. The scar looked ancient. Of the branch itself, which she had seen so clearly only minutes earlier, there was not a trace.

6

Kyle Montcrieff lay his knife and fork down on the plate, but didn't push them together. He was hoping there were seconds. The baked peppers with garlic, tomatoes and anchovies had been tasty but not very filling. Even though he'd eaten a whole round loaf of ciabatta bread with it, Kyle was still hungry.

His mother noticed the cutlery. "There's lots of fruit," she said, with an airy gesture towards the bowl at the end of the table.

Kyle sighed. He loved his mother and father dearly and often thought about them during term-time, but when he was home, he didn't half miss his school dinners. Steak and kidney pies and puddings, lamb stews with dumplings, doughy lasagnes and mountains of mash. And for afters! Syrup pudding, chocolate pudding, jam roly-poly and spotted dick, all drenched in thick, sweet custard. Travers College Boarding School was renowned for the stodginess of its meals. No one ever left the table feeling hungry there, and it was no coincidence that the school had won the Rugby Union County Cup for the previous three years.

Kyle played loose-head prop, so it was important for him to maintain his weight. Not that he was fat – circuit training in the gym and daily cross-country runs with a weighted knapsack on his back saw to that. He was, as Coach Brewster was fond of saying, built like a brick shithouse. The last time he'd gone back to school after the summer break though, he'd lost ten pounds. And no one wanted that to happen again – not for the beginning of the new season. He reached over, pulled a hand of bananas from the bowl, peeled one and began chomping. And then a second. And a third. The skins piled up on his plate. His mother watched him, a faint smile playing on her lips.

"Good job they're cheap at the moment," she said.

Kyle grinned. "Bags of slow-release energy," he said. "Coach Brewster swears by them." He peeled a fourth banana.

"I was reading something about mice the other day, in one of the Sunday papers," Mrs Montcrieff said. "Apparently scientists have found that if you halve their daily intake of calories, you double their life expectancy."

"Oh, yeafff..." Kyle muttered. He swallowed and lay the fifth and final banana skin on his plate. "Well, I'm not a mouse."

Mrs Montcrieff smiled. "No dear, I suppose you're not." She reached forward, took Kyle's plate and stacked it on her own. "Anyway," she said, "I'm not sure I approve of all these experiments they do on animals. Apparently the latest thing is, they've bred mice that glow in the dark."

Kyle laughed.

"I kid you not," said his mum. "They've taken the – I don't know the technological word for it – the *glowing* gene from some kind of jellyfish, injected it into a mouse egg and produced a luminous mouse. They say it'll help with research into cancer." She paused. "Though for the life of me, I can't see how!"

"So what Sunday paper *are* you reading these days, then?" said Kyle.

"Pardon? I..." She laughed. "Oh, I see. No, I haven't started buying tabloids. Actually, it was a woman in the shop this afternoon who told me about the luminous mice. I can't think how we got on to the subject, but she was absolutely adamant it was true. Said they'd done it in Japan."

"Doesn't sound like the usual Bridgemorton

Help the Aged conversation," Kyle remarked. Whenever he'd helped his mother in the charity shop the talk had never moved far from the weather (either *dreatful* or *glooorious*) and the rising cost of staying alive.

"No, well, she wasn't from round here," said Mrs Montcrieff. "She's one of those travellers camped up on Marvis Ridge."

Kyle nodded. He'd forgotten all about the protests. The travellers had begun arriving in their trucks and buses shortly after Easter, just as he was going back to school for the summer term. So, he thought, they're still here.

"Of course Mrs Armitage isn't at all impressed," his mother was saying. "She wedges the door open whenever one of them comes in."

Kyle chuckled. Mrs Armitage, with her angular glasses and blue rinse, was an appalling snob.

"Then she flits around with an aerosol full of air freshener," his mother went on. "Except this morning, that is. We were out of it, so she used fly spray! Kept saying 'I could have sworn I saw a bluebottle!' Absolutely priceless."

Kyle laughed. "I bet the woman wasn't happy."

"No, she wasn't! She had a little boy with her. Took one of the scarves from the counter, she did, and wrapped it round his mouth and nose. And tore a strip off Mrs Armitage, too. Said that the chemicals in fly sprays had been proven to cause cancer. Actually, come to think of it, that's how we got on to the glowing mice..."

Kyle snorted. "Old hippy, was she?"

Mrs Montcrieff smiled. "You're beginning to sound like Mrs Armitage, dear," she said. Kyle scowled. "I'd say she was in her mid-thirties, and she was wearing a long batik dress. If that makes her an old hippy then, yes, I suppose she was."

"Oh, Mother!" said Kyle impatiently. "You know what I mean. These people... Anti-road improvement, anti-vivisection – anti-everything. Travelling from place to place, causing problems. Living off the dole..."

His mother stood up from the table and loaded the dirty dishes on to a tray. "She gets a lot less per week than we pay out for your school fees," she said quietly.

Kyle watched her, bemused, as she picked up the tray and headed for the door. It wasn't like his mother to sound – well, *political*. "Mother!" he said.

She turned. "Yes, dear?"

"Are you all right?"

"Never felt better," came the reply. She left the room. "But thank you for your concern."

Kyle followed her into the kitchen. "It's just that..."

Mrs Montcrieff put the tray down on the draining board and turned to face him. "Kyle," she said, "they say it takes something personal to happen before you see what's going on generally. Well, this *is* personal. I know we need to stop the lorries coming through the centre of town, but I don't want to see Marvis Ridge destroyed. It's somewhere I used to go to as a child, somewhere I used to take you when you were a little boy – and somewhere I hope to be able to take my grandchildren one day."

Kyle shrugged. "You can't have both—"

"That's the point," said Mrs Montcrieff. "On this occasion, you can. A perfectly good, environmentally friendlier tunnel has been proposed, and that is what I – and all the old hippies – would like to see built."

"A tunnel?" said Kyle. "It would be far more expensive."

"Perhaps," said Mrs Montcrieff, "but I think it is money we cannot afford *not* to spend. Once the Ridge has been destroyed, it will be gone for ever."

Kyle shuffled about awkwardly. "You seem to know an awful lot about it," he muttered. He was beginning to feel quite uneasy. It was as though his mother – dear old, daffy old Daphne Montcrieff – had been abducted while he'd been away at school, and replaced with someone altogether more radical.

His mother smiled. "I am *up in arms*," she said. "I think that's the term the local rag used." She opened a drawer, pulled a newspaper clipping from between the place mats and handed it to Kyle. It was an article from the *Morning Argus*.

Local Residents Join Bridgemorton Bypass Protest, the headline announced. Beneath it was a photograph of a crowd of banner-carrying demonstrators. In the bottom left-hand corner was his mother.

Kyle looked up, surprised. "You've actually been there," he said.

"Several times," came the reply. "And what's more," she said, a touch of defiance creeping into her voice, "I intend going up there again tomorrow. There's a rally every Saturday, and tomorrow's promises to be the biggest yet."

At that moment, Kyle heard the sound of a car crunching its way up the gravel drive. It was his father, back from the office. Mrs Montcrieff returned the article smartly to the drawer. "You needn't mention any of this to your father," she said.

Kyle grinned. "What if he asks where you're going?"

"I doubt he will. I think he's playing golf."

"But if he does?" Kyle persisted.

It was Mrs Montcrieff's turn to grin. "It's high time I paid your great aunt Eliza a visit," she said.

Kyle nodded thoughtfully. "Can I come too?"

7

Although he still hadn't secured the platform to the tree, Gary seemed in no hurry to climb up into the ancient oak for a second time. Willow couldn't blame him, and when he suggested paying Camp Didgeridoo a visit, she leapt at the chance to leave the menacing clearing once again. They spent all day there, helping out wherever they could.

While Crow's Nest Camp was home to Monty and his friends, who were living high up in the branches of the tallest trees, Camp Didgeridoo was the centre of the tunnelling operations. There were three tunnels, two of which were already complete. When the bailiffs and bulldozers arrived, four volunteers would chain themselves to concrete blocks deep beneath the ground. The third and most ambitious tunnel – Pooh Bear Tunnel – was still being built.

The main shaft was over thirty metres deep. At the bottom, it divided into two. One stretch extended to the north, the other to the south-east. Although the latter was already a hundred metres long, the former was proving more of a problem. The earth was sandy and there was the constant danger of roof-collapse. It was on this tunnel that Gary and Willow helped out.

They winched bagfuls of dirt up from the bottom of the shaft and scattered it in the woods. They sawed lengths of four-by-four and branches of silver birch to use as pit props. They didn't stop. There were rumours going round that the authorities were due to arrive at any time now and it was important that everything was made ready before then. Everything had to be done to prevent – or at least delay – the felling of the trees.

Or most of them, at any rate, thought Willow. There was one particular tree she wouldn't mind never seeing again.

All the while she winched and scattered and sawed, the recent events went round and round in her head. None of it made any sense. Could a tree truly be haunted? And if it was, then why had Gary, she and Blue had such widely different experiences?

She looked up from the log she was sawing, and wiped the sweat from her brow. "Gary," she said.

"Yep?"

"What exactly did you see up in the oak tree yesterday?"

"Oh, Willow!" he snapped. "You're not still on about that, are you? I told you, it was nothing."

"Then why haven't you been up to fix the platform yet?" she asked.

Gary shrugged. "I just haven't got round to doing it, that's all," he said sullenly.

Willow remained silent. When Gary got a nark on, you just had to wait for it to pass. It always did. And sure enough, ten minutes later, he spoke again.

"Why are you so interested to know, anyway?" he asked.

"Because I had an odd dream last night," she explained.

"A dream," Gary repeated.

"Well, a nightmare, really," said Willow, and went on to tell him everything she could remember. About the onion rings oozing blood. About the hanging man with his monstrous blood-red face. About the atmosphere that had made her sob with grief.

When she had finished, Willow looked up. She saw that Gary had laid his saw aside and was staring at her open-mouthed.

"I saw a figure hanging, too," he said, quietly.

"But he was wearing a black hood over his head. I couldn't see his face. And there was a placard stuck round his neck," he added, "with something Latin written on it." He looked puzzled. "But..."

"What?" said Willow.

"There *was* another figure, just like the one you described – all red and bloated. But it was only there for a moment. And it wasn't the only one. There were all sorts. Angry faces. Sad faces. Screaming and shouting faces. Men's, women's and children's faces. Person and person after person – until it settled on the hanging figure in the black hood." He paused. "It was like having your whole life flashing before your eyes. The only trouble was," he laughed, "it wasn't my life."

Willow nodded grimly. The succession of ever-changing images was something she was all too familiar with. She, too, had seen them when she was looking for Blue. It had been like channel-zapping before deciding on a particular programme, or flicking through a book until you came to the right page. What was more, she remembered, she too had glimpsed a figure in a black hood.

But what did it mean? she wondered. That the oak tree was home to not one but several spirits? That she and Gary had both seen a sequence of episodes from the past? That the history of the tree was somehow bound up in its branches? Willow realized she was letting her imagination run away with her.

"There's probably some perfectly simple explanation for it all," she said.

"Bound to be," said Gary.

"For a start, we're camped in a really damp place," she went on. "If it wasn't for the drought we'd be in the middle of a marsh, and marsh gas is well known to cause delusions."

"Will-o'-the-wisps and such like," said Gary, nodding. "And then there are the television transmissions," he went on. "There's a booster beacon just north of here. I saw it before we turned on to the bridleway."

"What of it?" said Willow, confused.

"Well," said Gary, "Curly Willis reckons that during freak weather conditions – exceptionally high pressure, like we've got now – people can pick up television signals."

Willow started giggling. "What, in their heads?"

"That's what Curly says," Gary said. "It's all to do with the amalgam in their teeth. The more fillings, the better the reception..."

Willow howled with laughter. "This is the same Curly Willis who believes gerbils are the most intelligent beings on earth, I take it? The Curly Willis who befriends rocks, and who claims that he can make himself invisible."

Gary, too, started chuckling. "Perhaps he's here as we speak," he said. He looked round. "All right,

Curly, old son?" he said, and shook hands with the air.

Willow picked up her saw and continued cutting the log. "You're a nutter, you are," she said affectionately. "A real nutter."

Away from the ancient oak tree, it was easy to make light of what had been going on. It was only later, when they had packed up for the day and returned to their campsite, that Willow began to feel anxious all over again.

"Gary! Willow!" Blue cried out as they emerged into the clearing. He raced towards them. "Look at my new dungees," he said proudly.

"They look brilliant, mate," said Gary. "Did Mummy get them for you?"

Blue nodded happily. "In the smelly shop," he said.

Willow laughed. Sara looked up from the fire she was cooking over. "Fly spray," she explained, and wrinkled her nose. "Still, they had some good stuff there."

"Did you get me anything?" asked Gary.

"I did," said Sara, as she flicked the sizzling vegetables over in the pan. "A genuine MA1 flight jacket. Two pounds, it cost, and it doesn't look as it it's ever been worn. And I got Willow some jogging pants and a sweatshirt with a hood. And a denim skirt for me. They're all in a bin liner inside the bus."

As they sat down to eat, Willow knew she should have been feeling better. Sara's stir-fry was delicious and the tracksuit was soft, snug and fitted perfectly. However, despite the hot food and warm clothes, Willow still felt cold. The shudders were worse than ever. Even Sara noticed.

"Do you think you're coming down with something?" she asked. "I'll make you a glass of hot cider with cinammon."

Willow nodded. "That would be nice," she said.

By the time the meal things had been cleared away it was already dark. Willow was tired. The unexpected day's work had worn her out, and the cider had made her drowsier still. The trouble was, Gary and Sara were playing cards in the bus and chattering away nineteen to the dozen. Willow knew she'd never get to sleep there.

She pulled herself to her feet and headed for the door. Sara looked up.

"Are you going to sleep in your tent tonight?" she said.

Willow nodded.

"Night, love," she said.

"And sleep well," she heard Gary say.

Willow turned round and smiled at him wearily. "I'll do my best," she said.

Having checked all round the tent for mozzies, Willow switched off her torch and lay down. The thought of spending the night outside was far from welcome. She felt exposed and vulnerable. Then again, the air-mattress was infinitely more comfortable than the hard, narrow bunk on the bus. She was asleep within seconds.

Outside the tent, a light wind set the nylon walls trembling. Inside, Willow's eyelids began to flicker.

8

The air crackled with expectation. The leaves turned back on themselves as a breeze got up, and black clouds rolled across the sky and over the moon. Willow muttered in her sleep and turned on to her side.

Faces were flashing in front of her: old faces, young faces, faces familiar and faces she had never seen before.

Circles within circles. Rings within rings.

It was like hurtling down a long corridor lined with portraits. A red and bloated one. A warty one. A hooded one.

Willow spun giddily, round and round. Now she was falling. Now she had stopped. Now she was falling again. The faces continued.

All at once, one of them loomed towards her and stared fixedly into her eyes. It was a man's face. A young man's face, half hidden in shadows. It came closer, and Willow felt the warmth of his breath on her forehead. The lips moved, and the man uttered a single word.

"Now."

At that moment, a blinding flash ripped through the air. For an instant, the man's face was lit up – bony, stubbled, lined beyond its years and, she realized with a gasp of horror, quite dead. Then it disappeared completely.

Willow cried out and sat bolt upright, immediately wide awake. Her heart was pounding fit to burst.

"It was just a dream," she whispered to herself. "Just a bad old dream."

But if the faces had been part of a dream, then the lightning which had woken her from it was real enough. And, as she sat peering into the darkness, the thunder suddenly broke – deafening, booming, crashing, like bombs exploding one after the other. Instinctively, Willow curled up into a tight ball and clasped her arms tightly round her head.

The ground trembled. The air shook. The wind grew stronger. It howled and whined through the forest. The great trees creaked and whispered. Lightning struck again and again, with the thunder that followed now drifting away into the distance, now coming closer again, as if the storm was circling overhead.

The air was charged. It crackled, it sparked. It was heavy with wetness. Yet there was no rain.

Willow uncurled and crawled out to look for herself. As she emerged from her shelter, the wind hit her with a ferocity that took her breath away. She clambered to her feet and watched, spellbound, as the sky lit up above her and the forest below was bathed in silver and blue.

Ahead of her stood the tree. Willow looked up. The mighty, ancient oak stood taller than any of the other trees around it, as vast and imposing as any Gothic castle. High above its uppermost branches, the clouds writhed and heaved and spat out bolt after bolt of lightning, which hurtled back down towards the tree.

Willow gasped. The storm *was* circling. And at its very centre was the oak tree itself.

She backed away nervously. Most of the jagged zigzags of lightning fizzled away to nothing high above her, yet the danger remained that one stray bolt might pierce the canopy and strike the forest floor. She ducked down behind a low rock and crossed her fingers.

At that moment – and without any warning – the rain began. Huge spots spattered noisily against the leaves. Within seconds it had become torrential – blinding sheets of driving rain that rippled in the lightning flashes. Willow was soaked to the skin. Below her bare feet, the earth turned into a quagmire. Wet and cold, she remained where she was, crouching down beside the rock, too terrified to move.

And then she heard it, faint at first, but getting louder by the second – horses' hoofs. "Steady, girl!" came an angry voice, followed by the crack of a whip and the sound of anguished whinnying.

Horses? Willow wondered. *Here?* She looked round, and cried out as she saw a horse-drawn carriage hurtling towards her. The front lamps flickered between the tree trunks as it came closer and closer. And closer still...

At the last possible moment, Willow leapt back into the undergrowth. The horses drew level – eyes rolling, mouths frothing. One of them reared up.

"Easy!" yelled the driver, a bull of a man, as he pulled back hard on the reins.

The horse dropped back down on all fours and pawed at the ground. The carriage lurched to a halt. A man's head appeared at the window, jowly, bewigged and red with rage.

"Damn you, Smeal!" he roared. "Call yourself a driver?"

"The 'orses been spooked bad, m'lord," the driver replied. "Can't move 'em. I—"

The carriage suddenly pitched to the right as two more of the horses reared up. Lightning flashed, and Willow saw a man jump out from the shadows and stand before the carriage. The lamplight glowed on his raised hands, his two primed muskets, his rain-drenched face. Willow gasped.

It was the man she had seen in her dream.

"Your money or your life, Mayor Fothergill!" he bellowed, his voice breaking with fury or fear – or both.

For a moment, there was silence. The mayor looked the man up and down. "Thomas Marley," he sneered. "We meet again."

"Aye," came the reply. "And if you try anything clever, it'll be for the last time. Throw down your valuables. Now!"

He thrust the muskets forward menacingly. Mayor Fothergill merely smirked. "Why do you do it, Thomas?" he asked coldly. "Why do you think you have the right to take from your betters? Eh?"

"I'm not here to bandy words with you," Marley spat. "We'll get this over with quick."

"Oh, but Thomas," the mayor said, a wheedling edge coming into his voice "if this is to be our final encounter, I would so dearly like to understand."

As Willow watched Thomas Marley's pale and bony face twitch uncomfortably, she was seized by a feeling of tearful despair. She no longer wondered what the horse-drawn carriage was doing there in the middle of the night, or why it was being held up by a man dressed as a highwayman. The sadness was so overwhelming, so palpable, that every other thought abandoned her.

Abruptly, Marley's bewildered expression changed to one of defiance. "For my family," he said. "A wife and six children, I've got. And no means of supporting them. Leeches like you have bled me dry."

"Is it my fault you have chosen to breed like rabbits?" the mayor demanded contemptuously.

Tom glared back furiously. So did Willow. How could he say such a thing? Wasn't the family all that anyone had? As if echoing her own thoughts, Tom Marley spoke.

"I'll do anything I have to do for my family," he said. "Anything at all." He jerked the muskets. "Now throw down those valuables."

"That your family might grow big and strong?" the mayor sneered. "I don't think so."

Willow watched the rolls of flab around the mayor's neck quiver with amusement. Rage, blind rage, gripped her body.

Suddenly everything began to speed up. The mayor threw back his head and cackled with laughter. The driver turned. The horses stamped their hoofs and tossed their heads. Alarmed by the sudden flurry of activity, Thomas Marley spun round, muskets raised – and fired.

The driver slumped forwards. The panic-stricken

horses neighed and tossed their heads but did not bolt. Blood trickled down from the foot-plate.

The sky crackled, grew bright and faded again. Thunder tumbled all round.

Willow stared in horror at the body. Tom Marley let his arms fall limply to his side.

"Smeal had a family too," the mayor shouted. "A wife, three daughters and a son. Is your family so much more important than his?"

"To me it is," Willow found herself whispering. Yet even as the words left her lips she was overcome with a feeling of such unutterable grief that it hurt. She turned towards Tom Marley.

He was staring at the smoking muskets in disbelief. There were tears streaming down his face. "I would not ... I never intended ... I did not mean to..." he said, choking with a numbing remorse that could not express itself.

"Oh, stop that pathetic whining," the mayor snapped. "Guards! Seize him!"

All at once, there was a brief flurry of movement at the back of the carriage, and four soldiers emerged as if from nowhere. Willow gasped. They had been concealed in the trunk of the carriage for just such an eventuality. She watched helplessly as Marley was knocked to the ground with a savage blow from a flintlock rifle.

"String the bastard up!" the mayor screeched.

The soldiers stepped forward and dragged him to his feet. Marley made no effort to resist.

Willow's head spun with the speed and horror of it all. She felt scared, confused – and paralyzingly sad. The storm fizzed and flashed above her head, and in the rumble of the thunder that followed she heard clamouring voices. "An eye for an eye," they wailed. "A tooth for a tooth."

At the oak tree, Tom Marley stood passively waiting for the soldiers to secure the hanging rope from the big, broad, horizontal branch. His face betrayed not a trace of emotion but Willow knew what he was feeling. She could feel it herself: the abject regret for hurting the driver's family, the utter desolation of destroying his own. Wave after wave of clammy grief poured down over her. Tears welled in her eyes. The lump in her throat would not be swallowed away.

The noose was placed around Marley's scrawny neck. Willow chewed her lower lip as she saw the rope biting into the straining tendons.

The hurt, the pain, the sadness in her head would not go away, would not dissolve.

Marley's bony wrists were tied behind his back.

Two families ripped apart.

"A life for a life," the voices jeered.

The soldiers took the strain on the rope. The command to *pull* was given. Abruptly, the noose tightened. Willow's heart missed a beat as Thomas

Marley was jerked off his feet and hoisted up into the air. He didn't struggle. He didn't make a sound.

"No!" Willowed howled. "*No!*"

Suddenly, she was running. Above her head, the sky continued to glow and fade, the thunder rumbled ominously. Ahead of her, with its back towards her, the body of Thomas Marley dangled from the rope.

It was madness of course. After all, what could she actually do? Something. Anything.

Faster and faster, Willow ran. The forest flashed past in a blur, yet the body came no closer. All round her, the trees began to shimmer and spin, until she was speeding down a long green tunnel so fast her feet barely touched the ground.

The air became thick with the voices sneering and jeering, mocking her puny attempts to change what had happened.

"What's done is done," they whispered, "but you can join us if you wish."

"No!" she screamed. "Leave me alone!"

"You have come and you shall stay," the whispers persisted. "F'r ever 'n' ever!" chirruped a young voice. "But not *that* way," another voice cackled. "*This* way, *this* way," they cried out together. "*This* way!"

Willow stopped in her tracks. The voices were coming from behind her. Her head pounded. Her heart thumped. She turned round slowly, anxiously, scarcely daring to look.

And as she turned, so too did the body on the rope.

Willow found herself staring at the hanging corpse of Thomas Marley. She screamed. His face was blood-red now, his eyes bulged bloodshot in their sockets. She screamed again. The tongue purple and swollen was lolling from the side of his mouth.

She covered her eyes with her hands, but the hideous vision would not be shut out. "I'm sorry!" she cried out. "Believe me, I'm so, so sorry!"

And then it was over.

The atmosphere sweetened, softened. The tension was released. Willow opened one eye slightly and peeked out. The shimmering green was still there, but the hanging man had gone. She opened both eyes and gasped with surprise.

She was in her tent. A beam of sunlight was beating down on the green nylon wall. She rolled over, pulled the door-zip quickly up and stuck her head and one arm outside. She poked at the ground. It was dry, parched. There had been no rain. Not a drop.

"A nightmare," she said, scarcely able to believe that the words could be true. It had all been so vivid. Even now, the remnants of sadness clung to her as an awful memory. Thomas Marley had only acted to help his family, yet he had destroyed two families – the coach driver's and his own – in the process.

She thought of Blue, of Sara and Gary, of Roy. *Her* family. *Wasn't the family all that anyone had?* she thought, and wondered why the words seemed so familiar.

"The family," she whispered, trying hard to hold on to the feeling of the dream. But it was hopeless. The more wide awake she became, the further away it slipped.

Willow sat up, wriggled out of her sleeping bag – and screamed.

"No!" she gasped. "It isn't possible. It – it *can't* be!"

But it was. Her tracksuit was soaking wet. So was her hair. And her feet were caked with thick, gluey mud. Willow slumped forward, head in hands, and groaned.

"What is happening to me?" she said, her voice trembling with quiet desperation. "What is going on?"

9

Kyle's mother had been right about her husband on both counts: he was playing golf that Saturday, and he didn't ask her what she was planning on doing. All the same, Kyle felt a twinge of wrongdoing as he climbed up into the Range Rover beside her.

"Father would go bananas if he knew where we were going," he said.

"Well, I don't intend telling him," she said. She started the engine and set off down the driveway. "Yet."

Surprised, Kyle looked round at her. "You mean you will sometime?"

"When the time's right," she said, as she turned out into the road and changed gear. "I don't believe in keeping secrets," she continued thoughtfully. "I never have. But your father's the type of person who needs to have a situation presented to him properly. In due course, I'll be able to do that. And then ... well, he'll rant and rave at first, no doubt. But eventually he'll come round. He always does."

Kyle turned away. As far as he was concerned, William Gabriel Montcrieff was the most stubborn person he had ever known. He had never known his father to "come round" to anything. Still, presumably his mother knew best. He sighed, and turned his attention to the countryside speeding past outside.

Even Kyle, who took little notice of such things, could see that it was unnaturally dry. The grass at the roadside was yellow and brown, the trees were already shedding their leaves, the fields were full of wilting crops. The River Mor – where he had fished so often as a child – was low and sluggish. And although it was only half-past nine, the sun was already blazing down fiercely.

Global warming had all seemed a bit of a laugh to Kyle and his friends at Travers – something to be welcomed, not feared. It meant tennis and cricket matches were never rained off. It made outdoor swimming a joy rather than a chore. And they all cracked jokes about keeping the aerosols spraying so that the fine weather might continue.

Now Kyle could see the other side of it all. The down side. Dead crops. Dead trees. Dead fish.

"Did you know parts of the country are now officially classified as semi-arid by the UN?" his mother commented.

"I can belive it," said Kyle.

They drove on in silence, past dried-out ponds, withered plants and bushes, and huge swathes of land blackened by fires which had broken out in the tinder dryness. Glancing in the wing-mirror, Kyle saw clouds of dust boiling up behind them.

They came to a small crossroads and, turning left, passed by a place Kyle remembered well. There had been a shallow reedy pool in the middle of a stream, and when he was nine or ten, he had cycled there often to find newts, frogs and toads. These he'd put into glass jars and taken back to the pond in the back garden.

"Frog Corner!" he exclaimed.

Mrs Montcrieff slowed down and looked back. "Not any more," she said.

Kyle sighed. She was right. The stream had long since gone, and the pool – reedless now – was a dusty bowl, criss-crossed with cycle tracks.

"It's the amphibians which are taking the brunt of it all," she said as she set off again. "They're the creatures most sensitive to changes in the environment. Our barometer," she added, and snorted. "The natterjack and marsh frog are all but extinct. The common frog and toad are common only in name, and those that still exist are in a sorry state, spontaneously changing sex because of the levels of oestrogen in the water. Generating extra limbs. Failing to metamorphose properly. Producing sterile spawn."

Kyle remained silent. The facts were shocking, but what shocked him even more was his mother's detailed knowledge of the subject. She really *had* changed.

"Four hundred million years, they've been on earth," she went on. "Four hundred million years since they first crawled out of the primordial mud. And within the last decade their numbers have fallen by over fifty per cent." She shook her head and heaved a sigh of utter hopelessness. "We're killing the planet, Kyle," she said. "We're destroying our home."

Kyle shuffled round awkwardly in his seat. He still didn't know what to say. That she was exaggerating? That she was doom-mongering? That everything would turn out all right in the end? He knew how she would react. The silence between them grew strained as they continued along the winding country lane, and was broken only by a sudden series of dips in the road, caused by the contraction and subsidence of the clay underneath, which sent them bouncing up and down in their seats.

"Whoah!" they both cried, and laughed out loud.

Mrs Montcrieff gripped the wheel and gritted her teeth as the road grew worse still. The surface was cracked and pocked with potholes. One was so deep that she had to drive the car halfway up the far bank to get round it.

"Is this the only way there?" Kyle asked.

"It's the only way without road-blocks," his mother replied grimly. "They seal off all the main roads at the weekend. Mindless lackeys!" she spat. Kyle smiled to himself. This new version of his mother was so unlike the old version. Intrepid, defiant, outraged – all in all, a vast improvement! "Soon be there," she said. "Look to your right when we round the next corner."

Kyle did as he was told. Ahead of him, he saw a wide sloping hill filled with parked cars and trucks. Beyond that, a crowd of people. And beyond that – much to his mother's obvious annoyance – a line of police. At the top of the slope was the woodland of Marvis Ridge itself. Kyle stared in amazement. The whole place was thronging.

His mother turned right, on to a track between the fields, and headed towards it all. "Straight ahead of us is the main camp," she explained. "Camp Didgeridoo. The people there are tunnelling, I understand. And over there is Crow's Nest Camp," she said, pointing to her left. "Can you see? Near the top of the trees. There are about twenty of them living up on little platforms they've made high up in the branches. Day and night ... I think they're so brave." She gripped the gear lever and changed down. "And there," she said, nodding ahead of her, "that big marquee. It's the information centre. Various environmental groups have stalls there. David Rogers has spoken there."

"What, that nature-programme bloke on telly?" said Kyle.

Mrs Montcrieff nodded. "And they're hoping that explorer – oh, what's his name? The one who walked across Antarctica last year..."

"Miles Attley," said Kyle.

"That's the one," she said. "Well, he's expected. All sorts of people have lent their support," she said. "Film stars, pop stars, famous scientists, sportsmen and women." She laughed. "We've even had a member of the royal family," she added, and stole a furtive glance at her son.

"What?" said Kyle. "Not—"

Mrs Montcrieff nodded. "Himself!" she said. "In person. He shook my hand."

Kyle laughed. "You old fraud!" he said. "There was me thinking you'd turned into a revolutionary, and all the time it was just an excuse to press a bit of royal flesh."

"The Prince and I share an interest in environmental concerns," she said curtly, as she swung the car round into the lower field, parked and pulled on the handbrake. She turned to Kyle and burst out laughing. "Kyle dear," she said, "you must allow your mother her little foibles. That's what growing old is all about! Come on, then. Let's go and see what those nice policemen want," she said, smiling sweetly at her son. "I do hope they not thinking of denying us access to the camps."

Sara, Monty and Blue stood at the edge of the wood looking down at the rolling fields below them. There were more cars parked than usual, and a large crowd was milling about at the top end of the field.

"Here they come," said Sara dismissively, "the weekend protesters. Always assuming they get through the police line," she added. They reminded her of Roy, her ex. Like him, they had far too much respect for the law. "If the policemen tell them to go home, then home they'll go," she said.

"I wouldn't be so sure about that," said Monty. "Look!"

Some sort of a commotion was going on by the top gate. Voices were being raised. Arms were being waved in the air. Suddenly a woman burst through the line of police and began marching up the field. A tall, heavily-built youth came after her, followed by the rest of the crowd, as they poured through the gate and on up the hill. The policemen stood by awkwardly, unsure what to do next. A cheer went up all round the camp.

Monty laughed. "Never underestimate the determination of the green welly brigade," he said.

Sara remained unconvinced. "First whiff of trouble, and they'll be off again. We don't need them," she said. "We—"

"No, no," Monty interrupted, and shook his head. "I'm sorry, Sara, but you're wrong. We *do* need them. All *we* can do is draw people's attention to a situation, but we can't actually change anything. No matter how long a protest lasts, in the end the bailiffs move in and evict us."

"Yeah, but—"

"What we have to do is get public opinion on our side. And you don't do that by putting some spotty eighteen-year-old with dreadlocks and shaved bits in front of the camera to drone on about..." He turned on a particularly thick accent. "Like, I mean, all the the destruction and that, like, y'know..."

Sara smiled despite herself. "Monty, you old snob!"

"It's not a case of being snobbish," he protested. "Your average viewer will catch him on the news and think" – his accent became posh and clipped – "Oh, not another one of those dirty, scrounging, whingeing weirdos. A few years in the army – that's what he needs!"

Sara laughed. "So what's your point?" she said.

"That we all need to brush up on our 'how–now–brown–cows'? Or wear suits?"

Monty shook his head. "There's nothing more we can do," he said. "Our actions have persuaded them," he went on, waving an arm towards the approaching crowd of chattering men, women and children. "Now it's up to them to persuade the rest."

"But they only ever do something when it directly affects them," Sara persisted.

"You mean they're NIMBYs," Monty laughed. "Everything's OK as long as it's 'Not In My Back Yard'!"

"Exactly!" said Sara, expecting Monty to concede at least this point. But again he shook his head.

"Most of the country is *somebody*'s back yard," he said.

Sara nodded. He had a point. Still, the fact remained that at the end of the day the green welly brigade would all return to their nice homes, while she would have to make do with the mattress in the bus. Not that she wasn't happy with her own chosen lifestyle, but somehow it galled her to think that these were the people they needed to win over if their protest was to be successful.

"Penny for them," came a voice.

"Hiya, Willow!" said Sara. "Monty's just been telling me why I need to get a perm, a twin–set and some pearls."

"*And* a house," Monty chuckled.

"Otherwise, we won't get taken seriously," said Sara, and raised her eyebrows in exasperation.

Willow thought of all her fellow pupils at Mabelfield and shrugged. "Perhaps he's right."

"Oh, Willow!" said Sara with obvious disappointment. "Not you, too."

Willow turned away. She couldn't be bothered to get into the "us" and "them" argument again. "We've finished the platform," she said.

"Excellent," said Sara. "And how was Gary?"

"Fine. He reckons he's going to sleep up it from now on," said Willow. "We drilled holes in the four corners of the platform, threaded rope through, and tied it to the branches."

Sara nodded approvingly. "Much better than nails," she said. "We must respect the trees we're trying to save, or face the consequences."

"The consequences?" said Monty.

Sara explained how Gary had come over all dizzy and scared when he'd tried to nail the platform into place. "The oak tree is old," she said, "very old. And its spirit has become powerful. Naturally, it'll defend itself. It will resist any attempts to harm it."

Monty chuckled with amusement. "Good old Sara," he said. "Glad to see you haven't changed." And he looked at Willow for confirmation.

Willow smiled but said nothing. Much as she

hated to admit it, she had the horrible feeling that on this occasion her mum might be right.

By now, the crowd of local residents had made it up to the wood, where they had dispersed. Some had headed straight for the information marquee, some were talking to the travellers, most were standing around in silent clusters wondering what would happen next.

To the accompaniment of Red Indian whooping, the police had followed them up the hill. Now, still in a line, they stood in the field directly below the trees, hands behind their backs.

"They can't be going to evict us today, anyway," Monty observed.

"How do you know?" said Willow.

"No riot gear," he said, and they all laughed – all, that is, except for Blue, who was bored. "Hey, Blue," said Monty, and crouched down in front of him. "What does a pig put on cuts and blisters?"

"I don't know," said Blue.

"Oinkment," said Monty, and burst out laughing again. Willow and Sara smiled. Blue remained stony-faced.

"Mummy," he said, pulling at Sara's skirt with one hand and pointing with the other, "it's the woman in the smelly shop."

Sara looked round. "So it is," she said. "Clever

boy." The woman waved. Sara waved back. The woman started walking towards them.

"My cue to get back to Crow's Nest," said Monty.

"Monty! You hypocrite," said Sara.

"I said we needed them," he said, "not that I wanted to meet them."

"But she's very nice," Sara whispered.

"I'm sure she is," said Monty. "See you all later." And with that he was gone.

"Hel-lo!" the woman said brightly. She looked at Willow, then back at Sara. "Perfect fit, I see."

"Yes ... yes, they are," said Sara. "This is Willow, my daughter. And this is Blue," she said, trying to hold the squirming little boy still. "My son."

The woman offered her hand to Sara and Willow in turn. "Daphne Montcrieff," she said. "And this is *my* son," she said, "Kyle." He, too, reached out his hand.

"Pleased to meet you," he said to Sara. "Pleased to meet you, Willow. How's it going?" he boomed.

Willow smiled awkwardly. Although Kyle looked about the same age as her, he came over as much older. Self-possessed, self-confident. Public school, probably, she thought scornfully.

"So what's the latest?" Mrs Montcrieff asked Sara.

"Not much has changed," she said. "Pooh Bear Tunnel's still causing problems. Erm, the Under

Sheriff apparently has eviction notices ready but hasn't yet served them. . ."

Mrs Montcrieff looked away guiltily. Certainly the notices would not be served that morning: the Under Sheriff was, at that moment, playing golf with her husband.

"Oh, yes," Sara said with a grin. "And Miles Attley has confirmed." She looked around. "He may even be here now."

Mrs Montcrieff patted her handbag. "I brought my camera with me," she said. She linked her arm through Sara's. "Come on, dear," she said. "Let's see if we can find him."

Blue looked up at Willow. "What is *my exactly*?" he said.

"Miles Attley," Kyle laughed. "He's an explorer," he said. "He walked right the way across the South Pole. Just him and a pack of huskie dogs."

Blue nodded. Then, without waiting to hear any more, he turned on his heels and ran after Sara.

Kyle laughed and turned to Willow. "Now, do you think I inspired him to go and see our national hero – or did I frighten him off?"

"Bit of both, I should think," said Willow.

"And what about you? Do you want to see his talk?"

Willow shook her head. "Not particularly," she said.

"Me neither," said Kyle. He put his hands on his hips, breathed in and surveyed the scene all round him. "Tell you what, though," he said, "I wouldn't mind looking round." He fixed Willow with his clear blue eyes. "Fancy showing me the sights?"

Willow shrugged non-commitally, hoping he would take the hint and leave her alone. He didn't. But then he wouldn't, would he? Willow thought irritably. He was a typical public school type. Thick-skinned and pushy.

"Well?" he said brightly, a big, silly grin splashed all over his face.

Willow smiled despite herself. "OK," she said. "Where do you want to start?"

"You're the expert," said Kyle. "I'll leave it up to you."

10

Willow felt a fraud showing Kyle round the protesters' encampment. Expert? She'd only been there for two days herself. Still, in that time she'd learnt the whereabouts of most of the things of interest, and what she didn't know she wasn't afraid to bluff about.

She took him to see the three tunnels in Camp Didgeridoo, and introduced him to some of her friends. Gary was busy sawing wood again for the troublesome Pooh Bear tunnel.

"All right, Kyle?" he said, without looking up.

"Sound," said Kyle. "How's it going?"

Gary frowned. "I'm not too sure," he admitted. He laid the saw aside. "They're having real problems with that northern tunnel."

"Who's down there?" asked Willow.

"At the moment, Curly and Mole," said Gary.

Kyle nodded earnestly. "Serious business, tunnel digging," he said. "What's the point of it all?"

Willow cringed.

Gary looked at him as though he was simple-minded. "To delay the tree-felling," he said. "They can't bring the bulldozers in until the site's been cleared – above ground and down below."

"Of course," said Kyle. "And these problems?"

Gary shook his head. "All I know is, Steg emerged from the entrance about half an hour ago, white as a sheet and shaking like a leaf."

Willow shivered with foreboding. She knew that the northern tunnel led back towards the place where the woods were at their densest, where Sara had decided she wanted to set up camp – where the ancient oak tree grew. "Do you know where Steg is now?" she asked.

Gary shook his head. "Not sure. He probably went off to find Tashie. And she's over at Crow's Nest."

"I'm going to see if I can find him," said Willow to Kyle. "You don't have to come with me."

"Oh, that's all right," Kyle assured her. "Don't mind me."

Willow groaned. That was just it – she did mind. The trouble was, there wasn't much she could do short of telling him to get lost, and she wasn't certain that even that would work.

Resigning herself to the situation, Willow headed westwards along the top of the ridge, with Kyle tagging along beside her. They passed a group of children playing cards on a blanket, a woman beading another woman's hair, three young men lying around listening to the industrial hammerblow of electronic dance music blaring out from a ghetto blaster. Willow smiled to herself as she wondered what the public schoolboy was making of it all. Suddenly, her smile froze.

Just up ahead, a wiry young man with a greasy bandanna tied round his head was sitting on the steps of a caravan, strumming a guitar and humming tunelessly. Willow groaned. The man's name was Sleaze. She had never liked him.

Sleaze had shifty eyes that never met your gaze, and when he spoke a sneer played constantly round his lips. Whenever they met up – on rallies, sit-ins, protest marches – Sleaze would always try to chat her up, entice her inside his filthy caravan. Willow had been appalled to learn that there were rumours going – started, no doubt, by Sleaze himself – that he and she had something going on.

As they approached him, Willow slipped her arm through Kyle's and smiled up at him. Although surprised, Kyle made no effort to pull away. Slight, blonde and blue-eyed, Willow was everything that Kyle had fantasized about a thousand times at Travers. He smiled back at her.

Sleaze looked up and stopped strumming. He sneered at Willow, at Kyle.

"Sleaze, Kyle. Kyle, Sleaze," said Willow as they went by.

"How's it going?" boomed Kyle.

Willow flinched, but kept hold of Kyle's arm. Sleaze nodded back suspiciously.

"Cool," he whined.

Willow flinched for a second time. Just the sound of his voice gave her the creeps. Physically, she knew she was more than equal to him, yet there was something menacing about Sleaze that unnerved her. With Kyle by her side, however, she felt completely safe.

"Catch you later, Willow," Sleaze called after them. "Maybe we could chill out together."

"Yeah, maybe," she said, and added, when she was sure he was out of earshot, "in your dreams." She turned to Kyle and grimaced. To her surprise, Kyle broke into a deep, throaty laugh. "What?" she said.

"Nothing," said Kyle. "I ... Oh, I don't know. I thought... You know, hippies and all that. I thought..."

Willow frowned and pulled her arm away. "Peace, love and get your knickers off, you mean," she said.

"Well, not quite, but..." Kyle said.

"I'm second generation hippy," she said primly.

"Part of the backlash. I yearn for gravy boats and napkin rings." Kyle frowned with puzzled amusement. "Anyway," Willow said, "Sleaze isn't my type."

As she said it, Willow wondered precisely what *was* her type. If anyone had suggested, even an hour earlier, that it might be a great big rugger-bugger kind of bloke she'd have laughed out loud. It was perplexing, therefore, to find just how excited she had felt walking arm in arm with him. There was something thrillingly reassuring about his big, solid body. Even if her head told her that Kyle Montcrieff was a no-no, her body was beginning to have doubts.

She stole a glance at him. Their eyes met. She looked away again, hoping that she didn't look quite as pink as she felt, and went through everything she'd seen, from top to toe, as if scrutinizing a photograph.

Thick, dark brown hair. Wavy. Unruly. A straight nose. A slight cleft in the chin. A neat little ear. A grey sweatshirt, big and loose, but failing to conceal the muscular bulk of his body. A small knapsack. Dark blue shorts. Long legs. Expensive trainers.

Is he really good looking? she wondered. I mean, would other girls look at him and go *fwooah!* – or is it just me?

"This bloke, Steg," he said, as they walked on. "Why do you want to see him?"

Why, are you jealous? thought Willow, and groaned inwardly. Get a grip! she told herself. "I wanted to find out what frightened him," she said.

Kyle nodded. "White as a sheet and shaking like a leaf," he said. "Must have been something pretty bad."

"Yes," she said. "I've..." Willow paused. If she started talking about the oak tree and the curious goings on, Kyle would think she was round the twist. "There's been a couple of other odd happenings," she said vaguely. "People being frightened. Saying they've seen things. I wondered if..."

Kyle nodded again, but said nothing.

Dammit, thought Willow. I've blown it. "Nearly there," she said brightly, eager to change the subject. "Look."

Ahead of them was the first of the tree-dwellers. High up in the branches of an old ash tree, like a giant cocoon, was a sleeping bag hanging up to air. Beside it, a hunched figure was sitting on a platform, leaning back against the trunk, reading.

Kyle stopped, put his hands on his hips and whistled with admiration. "That's high!" he said. "And look at those rope walkways connecting the trees." He shook his head. "Must have taken some nerve to string them across."

Willow called up into the first tree. "Hello, up

there!" A familiar face looked down. "Oh, hiya, Crimper!" she said. "Have you seen Tashie?"

"She went off with Steg about half an hour ago," the reply floated down. "I don't know where. Who's your friend?" she added.

"The name's Kyle," Kyle called back. "Kyle Montcrieff. How's it going?" he boomed.

On hearing those three little words once again, Willow sighed. It could never work. Kyle might look like a hunk, but he sounded like a prat.

Up above, Crimper rattled the chains that had been secured round the tree. "All ready to do my Emily Pankhurst bit when the bailiffs come."

Willow laughed. "If you see either of them, can you tell them I'd like a word with Steg?" said Willow, as she led Kyle away.

"Will do," Crimper called after them.

There were twenty-four occupied trees in all, spread throughout the woods. Some of the tree-dwellers Willow knew, most she did not. Kyle didn't seem bothered either way. Every time they passed a tree with someone in it, he smiled up cheerfully, waved and asked them how it was going. Willow grew more and more embarrassed.

It was about fifteen minutes later when she finally spotted Monty – or rather Monty spotted her. He was high up in a sycamore tree set back from the edge of the ridge. Willow introduced the pair of them and Kyle, inevitably, bellowed his "How's it going?" up into the branches.

A broad grin spread over Monty's face. Having gone to public school himself, he recognized the greeting only too well. "Boarding school?" he said.

"Travers College," Kyle nodded.

"Rugger?" said Monty.

"Loose-head prop," said Kyle.

"Extra-curric?" said Monty.

"Boxing. Middle-weight."

"Any good?"

Kyle lowered his head modestly, and shuffled about. "Not bad," he said.

Willow nodded to herself. She'd got Kyle absolutely spot on: the school, the rugby – and the boxing came as no surprise. She also knew what it all meant: *he* was posh, *she* was a pleb. And every time either of them opened their mouths these two facts would be reinforced.

"Why don't you come up?" Monty called. "It's an amazing view." And he let down a rope ladder from the platform.

"After you," said Kyle.

Willow hesitated. "Actually, I don't think I'll bother." A look of disappointment flickered across Kyle's big, open face. "But I'll wait if you want to go up," she said.

Kyle grinned. "I won't be long," he said, and with that, he turned to the rope ladder and began climbing. Hand over hand he went, foot after foot. With his forearm and calf muscles tensing and relaxing rhythmically, he made light of the awkward rope rungs. He reached the branches and continued up towards the platform where Monty was waiting, hand outstretched to help him up the last bit.

Kyle looked down at Willow and waved. He wasn't even red in the face. "The view really is fantastic," he boomed. "Over there is the cathedral," he said, pointing. "And over there, I can see the sea. It's incredible! Are you sure you don't want to come up?"

"Yeah, I'm sure," said Willow. She smiled to herself. He was just like a big kid. The next moment, she gasped. Although unable to make out what Monty and Kyle were saying, she could see what they were doing.

"You be careful," she called up, as Kyle swung away from the platform and on to the rope walkway connecting the sycamore to a neighbouring silver birch.

"Yes, Mother," Kyle boomed back and laughed.

Willow winced. First with Gary, now with Kyle. Why couldn't she ever keep her mouth shut? All the same, as he made his way along the two parallel ropes – one for his hands and one for his feet – she felt sick with anxiety. It was a twenty-metre drop down on to a ground littered with rocks, and there he was, bouncing around on the ropes like a gorilla.

Willow couldn't look. She turned away and walked off slowly, humming to herself agitatedly.

"Hey, Willow!" came a booming voice. "Wait for m—aaaarggh!"

Willow spun round. "Oh, God," she murmured.

He was falling, falling, spinning down from above.

"Kyle!" Willow screamed and raced towards him.

"Wheeeee!" went Kyle.

Wheeeee? Willow stopped. She saw the rope woven round his back and between his feet. He wasn't falling at all. He was abseiling.

"You bastard!" she screamed, and began running all over again. Kyle slowed himself down on the rope and landed softly on his feet. He was grinning from ear to ear. Willow was there to meet him. She hurled herself at him furiously.

"What?" Kyle laughed, fending her off gently. "What is it?"

"I thought you'd really fallen," she said angrily, and kicked savagely at his exposed shins.

Kyle jumped back safely out of the way. "I'm sorry," he said. "It was a stupid thing to do."

"Yes, it was," said Willow. "A bloody stupid thing to do." Suddenly it all became too much for her. Gary and his hooded ghost. Blue and the two naughty boys. The hanged man of her own nightmares – as well as whatever it was that had so frightened Steg. She burst into tears. There was something horribly wrong at the heart of Marvis Ridge. Something unfinished, yet impending. Something evil. And here was this – this pumped up, jumped up, overgrown schoolboy pretending to fall out of a tree. "You idiot!" she sobbed, but the anger in her voice had disappeared.

She felt Kyle's arms around her. Warm, strong, reassuring arms. "I really am sorry," he whispered.

Willow sniffed and pushed him away. "I over-reacted," she said. Her heart was racing.

"No, you—"

"I did," she said, and wiped her eyes on her sleeve. "And I'm sorry, too." She sniffed again, and smiled. Something had occurred to her. "So, how can I make amends? How about a cup of coffee back at my place?"

Kyle nodded eagerly, happy that Willow no longer seemed to be angry with him.

"It's this way," she said.

"See you around, Monty," Kyle boomed back. "Catch up on how it's going."

Willow smiled to herself. Good old Kyle, she thought. Good old, brave old, confident old Kyle. Despite herself, she had to admit how agile he'd been up on the ropes, how fearless. Her tears had alarmed him far more than his aerial acrobatics.

It was for this reason that she had decided to invite him back to their campsite. Kyle was practical rather than emotional, with his feet – for the most part – planted firmly on the ground. She would show him the tree, tell him all about her bad dreams, and he would dismiss them as a lot of silly nonsense. That was what Willow wanted.

Yet when Kyle spoke, his voice sounded strangely subdued. "You're camped down here?" he said.

Willow looked at him. His face had drained of all colour. He was chewing his lower lip nervously.

"Yes," said Willow. "Why? What's the matter?" For a moment the whiff of garlic filled the air, and then was gone again as they trudged on down an ancient trough between the dense, dark undergrowth. "Kyle," she said, when he made no reply, "Kyle, you're frightening me. What is it?"

Kyle stopped. He turned and looked at her as though seeing her for the first time. "I've been here before," he said, "when I was little." He fell silent and stared round him suspiciously.

"And?" said Willow at last.

He looked back at her. His forehead furrowed, his blue eyes clouded with concern. "You won't laugh at me, will you?" he said.

Willow shook her head. "Of course I won't."

"Well..." He swallowed. "Do you believe in ghosts?"

11

Willow sighed unhappily. These weren't the words she wanted to hear – not from big, strong, meat-eating, middle-weight Kyle Montcrieff. They were bulgar wheat and muesli words. They were featherweight words. She hoped he was teasing her again. One look at his face, though, was enough to confirm that he was deadly serious.

"Well?" he said. "Do you?"

"Believe in ghosts?" said Willow. She wanted to know what he had to say before committing herself. "Why?" she asked.

Kyle shook his head. "You'll think I'm round the twist."

"I won't," Willow assured him, aware of how,

suddenly, the situation between them had been reversed. "Honest, I won't."

Kyle looked ahead and started walking slowly forwards. "Ten years ago, it happened," he said. "I was only seven years old, but I remember it all so clearly – as if it was yesterday."

Willow felt the shivers running up and down her back, as if an icy finger was playing arpeggios along her spine. She waited for Kyle to go on.

"Mother and father had brought me up to Marvis Ridge for a picnic." He frowned. "It was a sunny day, but there was a cold wind blowing on the ridge itself. Mother suggested we find somewhere more sheltered. In the woods." He looked round. "There was less bracken and stuff growing then. Anyway, we walked on – I don't know how far – until we came to a tree." He closed his eyes and shuddered at the memory. "A massive great oak tree."

Willow groaned with disappointment. She had been hoping against hope that his story would have nothing to do with the oak tree. Now those hopes had been dashed.

"So what happened?" she asked quietly.

Kyle took a deep breath. "We'd finished eating our picnic," he said. "Mother and Father were snoozing on the blanket. I was bored. I decided to climb the tree. I wanted to carve my name into one of the branches." He paused. "It went well at first but then things started to happen." His face clouded over. "Everything went fuzzy. And there was a tunnel. And faces and voices, and..." He turned towards Willow and shrugged.

"And?"

"And then I saw her," he said. "The witch. The wicked witch. Straight out of a fairy tale, she was, with long black hair and a hooked, warty nose. Lizzie, her name was. She ... she leant towards me and prodded me hard in the ribs. I keeled over and fell out of the tree. And all the time I could hear her cackling laughter." He went quiet, then added, "I've still got the mark." He lifted his sweatshirt and vest up. "Look."

Willow saw a small white scar, on the left of his chest. She smiled nervously. "Just above the heart," she said.

Kyle nodded and continued walking.

"Of course," said Willow, "you could have cut yourself in the fall."

"I know that," said Kyle. He sounded hurt. "I could have been suffering from concussion. I could have imagined the whole thing. But..." He looked at her earnestly. "It was all so real." He shuddered. "And ten years later I still get nightmares about that hideous old hag." He laughed. "There you are," he said. "Now tell me I'm a loony."

Willow stared back at him sympathetically. It was time for her to come clean about what she herself had seen. "No," she said. "I—"

But Kyle cut her short. "There it is," he said. His voice was low and quavery. He hadn't even noticed the bus parked in the shadows, or the tent. He strode forwards to the ancient oak tree and placed his hands tentatively against the gnarled bark. He turned back to Willow. "It's exactly as I remember it," he said.

Slowly, he inched his way round the massive trunk. Willow followed him. It was the first time she had been round to the back of the tree. There was a hole at the base of the trunk on the far side. It was large enough for both of them to climb inside, but neither of them did.

"How old do you think it is?" said Willow.

Kyle shook his head. "Hundreds of years old," he said. "Maybe a thousand. The only way you could tell for sure would be to cut it down and count the rings inside."

As he spoke, Willow trembled with sudden realization. "That's it!" she exclaimed.

"What?" said Kyle.

"The rings," she said, as she walked on around the tree. "The concentric circles. They weren't onion rings at all. They were the yearly growth rings – the rings of time."

Kyle turned. "What are you talking about?" he said.

"I ... I've seen things, too," she faltered.

Kyle stared at her in confusion. "You mean—"

"You asked me if I believed in ghosts. Well, the answer is yes," she said and, as they continued slowly round to the front of the tree, she told him everything that had happened to her and the others. Every single detail. Kyle listened in silence.

"So," he said, when she had finished, "you, me, Blue and Gary have all seen something."

"And maybe Steg as well," Willow reminded him.

The pair of them stared up into the branches of the tree. Then without saying a word, Kyle began climbing. Willow stared, open-mouthed. "What are you doing?" she whispered.

"I just want to see if I can find where I wrote my name."

"But—"

"It's all right," he interrupted, and looked down at her. "You said Gary tied the platform up with no problems, didn't you?"

"So?" said Willow.

"Well, it's obvious, isn't it? The tree only responds if it feels under threat," he said. "When I was cutting into the bark, when Gary was about to hammer his nails in, when your fire sent burning sparks up into its branches."

"Oh, yeah?" said Willow. She didn't like being talked to as though she was an idiot. "And what about Blue?"

Kyle shrugged. "He was probably up to

something or other. Come on," he said, reaching down with his hand. "We'll be fine."

Willow still wasn't sure. Then again, if something else was going to happen, she would rather it be when she was with Kyle than when she was on her own.

She stretched up, grasped Kyle's hand and heaved herself up beside him. Kyle went higher. Willow looked around. Everything was as it should be. So far, so good, she thought as she followed him up.

"Aha!" Kyle announced a moment later. "I've found it."

Willow pulled herself up beside him and looked down. There on the branch were three letters carved into the bark.

"KYL," said Willow.

"Kill?" said Kyle, and then realized what she had really said. "I didn't have time to finish it," he explained.

Willow nodded. "I know," she said uneasily. The missing E made all the difference to the word. She hoped it wasn't some horrible omen.

They continued up the tree, cocooned inside the dense foliage. Where no leaves grew, thick clumps of mistletoe hung down from the underside of the branches. They arrived at Gary's platform from different sides at exactly the same time.

"Not quite as plush as Monty's one," Kyle

commented. He stamped his feet down hard, "but solid enough. Is Gary planning on chaining himself up as well?"

"That was the idea," said Willow. She sat down. "There's a road just north of here, so this part of the forest is quite vulnerable. Once the eviction notice has been served, he's going to keep a permanent lookout. If the bulldozers come from this direction, he'll chain himself up and then blow his whistle for reinforcements."

Kyle grinned. "It all sounds pretty exciting," he said. "I envy you."

"Exciting?" Willow said, and snorted. "I suppose it is. But I'm sick of it. Sick of everything."

Kyle sat down opposite her. "I don't understand," he said. "I thought—"

"I'm sick of living in a bus," she said. "I'm sick of travelling from one good cause to the next. I'm sick of campaigns. I'm sick of protests. I'm sick of being evicted by bailiffs and guards and police with riot gear and big dogs, and..." She stopped, bit into her top lip. Her eyes were welling with tears. "And you envy me!"

Kyle stared at her helplessly. It was the second time he'd made her cry. He moved forward, crouched down next to her, hesitated – he didn't want to be pushed away again. Willow looked up. She saw his big, gentle, concerned face staring into hers. How weird it was, she thought, that he knew what she had been going through better than anyone else. She reached out towards him.

Relieved, Kyle smiled and opened his arms to her. They hugged. They kissed. They lay down on the platform, wrapped in each other's arms, and kissed some more.

The air trembled. The leaves glinted.

Willow opened her eyes and looked upwards. "Kyle!" she gasped.

"Mmmff?" he mumbled.

"Kyle!"

Shocked by the alarm in her voice, he pulled away and rolled over. All round them, the green was shimmering, blurring, breaking down into the countless pixels of scintillated light.

"This was it!" he cried. "This is what happened." He jumped to his feet and shouted into the branches. "But we haven't done anything!" he cried out. "We haven't hurt you."

The emerald shimmering continued, and rings began to form, just like before. Willow climbed shakily to her feet. She sought out Kyle's hand and squeezed it tightly. Circles within circles, rings within rings. All at once, the centre spun backwards, and Kyle and Willow found themselves staring down the long, shimmering green tunnel. Willow screamed.

She was falling. Falling down into the spinning vortex. She gripped Kyle's hand all the tighter, hoping that he might pull her back. Instead, with a cry of despair, he too tumbled down with her.

Faces leered, voices jeered and cackled as vision after fearful vision loomed up in front of them and was gone.

Terrified, Willow and Kyle clung on to one another as they fell.

The blood-red, bloated features of the hanging man loomed in front of them, tongue twitching, throat gurgling.

The warty, hook-nosed face of the witch zoomed in and out.

Another hanging man. And another.

And a burning woman.

One after the other. Fleeting, yet no less terrible for that.

A dangling man, his skin flayed raw.

A girl, the side of her head caved in, one eye hanging from its socket.

Retching with horror, Willow screwed her eyes tightly shut, but the gallery of terrifying portraits continued to flicker before her eyes. They grimaced, they gurned, they brought with them messages from the darkness.

"Join us in the Tree of Death," whispered one.

"Let us go, let us go, let us go!" wailed another.

"The tree is evil."

"Come to the tree. Come!"

And all at once the air was full with the

screaming and shouting of that single word – "Come! Come! Come!" – seven times in all. "Now!"

Then silence.

Willow opened her eyes again. She was back on the platform, holding Kyle's hand. She looked up at him.

"It's over," she said.

But Kyle did not reply. He had not heard her. He was staring intently in front of him. Mouth open. Eyebrows drawn together in confusion.

Willow glanced round. The trees, she saw, were still shimmering unnaturally. It wasn't over at all. With her heart in her mouth, she spun round. And there, hovering in mid-air, she saw the body of a young man. He was dressed in boots, jeans and a T-shirt, all covered in mud. He had long, matted dreadlocks. His face, blue-grey and smeared with mud, turned towards them.

Willow screamed. "No! No! It can't be!" she cried. "Oh, Kyle..." She struggled to get her breath. "Kyle," she said again, and swallowed, "I know him."

12

Willow tried to breathe more evenly, to quieten her thumping heart – but in vain. All she could do was stand and watch the frantic mime unfolding before her. The fingers grasping helplessly at the neck. The mouth gasping for breath. The eyes, filled with terror, staring round in blind desperation.

Then, imperceptibly at first, the figure began to fade. The colours became muted and the body dissolved away to nothing. Her head throbbed with impotence and frustration. There was nothing she could do. Nothing at all.

"Gone," she trembled, as the figure disappeared and the surrounding leaves stopped shimmering. "He's gone."

Kyle turned towards her. "You said you knew him."

Willow nodded. "I met him when I was eight or nine," she said, struggling to hold back the tears. "Up north. We were all trying to prevent a valley being flooded to make way for a reservoir." She paused, and smiled. "He used to make me garlands of flowers. Not just daisy chains, but proper plaited garlands. Like Hawaian leis. When they finally completed the dam I threw one on top of the rising water." She turned on Kyle angrily. "Because we failed to stop the reservoir, like we fail to stop everything else..."

Kyle looked away. He felt helpless in the face of such obvious distress.

"And now," she said, her voice quieter, "now this!" She sniffed and wiped her eyes.

"Who was he?" Kyle asked gently.

Willow took a deep breath. "It was Mole," she said.

"What, one of the tunnellers?" said Kyle.

Willow nodded. "Whatever it was that frightened Steg so badly must have ... killed him."

Kyle frowned. "Not necessarily," he said.

"What do you mean?" said Willow.

"Well, what if it was a warning?" he said. "What if we've just seen what could happen if we don't do something about it?"

For a moment, Willow remained silent as Kyle's

suggestion sank in. The next, she was shinning down the tree. "Come on!" she yelled. "If we're going to do something, it'll have to be now!"

Down, down, they both climbed hurriedly down through the branches and, with a final leap, landed together on the ground beneath. Then, without pausing to catch their breath, they leapt up and dashed off into the undergrowth. Past the tent and bus, they ran. (The guided tour could wait.) Up the steep track, through bracken and brambles – and a whiff of wild garlic – and back towards the top of the slope where it opened out into Marvis Ridge itself.

Willow stopped. She looked down at the encampment, then turned to Kyle. "It's no use," she panted. "We're too late."

Blue lights were flashing. The police were giving orders to the onlookers through loudhailers. A helicopter chugged overhead.

Kyle nodded miserably. Willow was right, and he felt awful for having raised her hopes in vain. "Do you want to go back to your bus?" he asked.

"What, and the tree?" said Willow. "You must be joking! No," she said, and sighed resignedly. "Let's go and see what's happened."

There were crowds of people there when they arrived, all milling about and talking in hushed, excited voices. People of every shape and description. Willow and Kyle mingled with them, catching snatches of their whispered conversations.

It was as though, just as Noah's Ark had gathered to it animals of every kind, so Marvis Ridge had attracted people from every walk of life. There were bikers and boffins and blue-rinsed ladies. Police teams and ambulance crews. Old people, young people, wealthy and poor people. Gentle and caring people. Mean, mad and media people. Celebrities. Nobodies... And one young man whose stretchered body was slowly being dragged back along the tunnel that had taken his life.

The whispers continued as Willow made her way through the crowd. She kept overhearing snippets of information – some true, some false. "Let me through," she said impatiently as, head down, she pushed past the knots of bystanders. "Let me through. I—"

Suddenly, someone was blocking her way. "Willow?" she heard, and felt a hand on her shoulder. She looked up.

"Steg!" she exclaimed, alarmed by his deathly pallor. "I've been looking for you."

"I know," Steg nodded. "Crimper told me." He sounded as drained as he looked. "What was it you wanted?"

"I ... I wanted to know what happened to you down in the tunnel," she said.

Steg snorted. "What, so you can laugh at me like Tashie did?" he said, swallowing back the tears. He shuddered. "Like Mole did..." He hung his head. "If only he'd listened to me..."

Willow reached forward and took him by the hands. "I won't laugh, Steg," she said. "I promise I won't. But you must tell me what you saw."

He looked up, his eyes filled with terror. "What I saw?" he cried. "I'll tell you what I saw. I saw right down deep into the bowels of hell. I saw torture and death. I saw evil – pure evil. And it saw me."

Willow shivered with unease. Steg was ranting. It was little wonder that Tashie hadn't believed him. But Willow did. She believed every word.

"What exactly do you mean?" she asked.

"I mean just what I say," he shouted. "It *saw* me! It knew I was there. I smelt its warm, putrid breath. I felt its bony fingers wrapping themselves around my neck. 'This is where you belong,' it whispered. 'Here with me – with us.' I heard it." His eyes glazed over. "It spoke to me. Evil spoke to me."

Willow stared at Steg helplessly. His whole body was trembling violently. She had never, ever seen anyone so terrified. "But you got away," she said gently.

"Got away," Steg repeated flatly. He shook his head, he took a deep breath. "God knows how," he said. "Suddenly I was scrabbling backwards. I had to escape. I just had to. I passed Mole. He was hammering a pit-prop into place. 'Get out of here while you still can!' I told him. But he just ... laughed." Suddenly, Steg's face crumpled. Tears streamed down his face. "And now look what's happened," he sniffed. "He's dead. Mole is dead." And with that, he spun round on his heels and dashed off, barging his way through the gawping crowds.

Willow turned to Kyle. She couldn't speak, but Kyle knew what she was thinking. He had let her down.

"I know," he said. "I'm sorry."

They continued walking in silence. Ten metres from the entrance to the now notorious Pooh Bear tunnel, a black and yellow strip of plastic which marked the edge of the cordoned-off area forced them to stop. Willow clutched the makeshift barrier and peered at the tunnel head, where four men were standing beside a winch system, arms folded, waiting.

"What's going on?" Willow asked a policewoman standing just to her left.

"Some accident underground," she replied without looking round. "One of them tunnellers."

"And is he all right?" said Willow, hoping against hope that the policewoman might even now tell her that he wasn't dead after all.

She turned. "Are you a relative?"

"He's my uncle," said Willow. It was almost true.

The policewoman moved towards her. She looked her in the eyes. "I'm so sorry," she said.

"But ... but what actually happened?" said Willow, her last glimmer of hope cruelly snuffed out.

"The information we have is sketchy," she said. "There was a collapse at the end of the tunnel." She paused. "It would have been very quick."

Willow nodded. She knew the woman was trying to be kind. She knew, too, that she was wrong. Mole's death had been as slow as it had been agonizing.

"And they haven't brought him up yet?"

The policewoman shook her head. "There are so many trapdoors and obstacles along the tunnel," she explained. "The rescue services have found it all but impossible to retrieve the ... the ... to get him out."

Willow nodded ruefully. "Uncle Mole always was very thorough," she said.

At that moment, a flurry of movement from the tunnel head caught their attention. Galvanized into action, the four men – two on either side – had each seized hold of the steel handles of the pulley wheel and were taking the strain on the ropes. A fifth man ran towards them, a mobile phone clamped to his ear.

"Wait. Wait for it," he said. Then, "Now!"

The four men started turning. Up down, up

down, they bobbed. Round and round went the wheel. Willow didn't want to watch, but couldn't make herself turn away. All round her, the crowd went silent as the men continued to raise their heavy load. As it came close to the top, there was a soft *bump, bump, bump!* as it knocked against the side of the hole. Then the corner of the stretcher appeared. Everyone gasped.

Willow watched, numb and disbelieving, as two of the four men secured the ropes, while the other two, together with the man with the mobile, manoeuvred the stretcher out of the hole and laid it down on the ground. He couldn't really be dead, she thought. He just couldn't. Not Mole!

Suddenly, without thinking what she was doing – and before either Kyle or the policewoman realized what was happening – Willow found herself ducking down under the black and yellow ribbon and racing towards him. The men looked up in surprise as she skidded to a halt at the stretcher, and knelt down beside it.

Mole's eyes were still open. She hadn't been expecting that. In fact, had it not been for the deathly pallor of his skin, he might have been simply resting, gazing up at the sky.

"Oh, Mole!" she whispered. "What happened to..." She froze. There was a twist of knotted wood wound tightly around his neck. He must have got tangled up in the roots, unless...

Willow trembled at the thought of the awful alternative – that his death had not been accidental. She lifted her head and gasped with horror. His gaze was fixed on hers. She stared back into his eyes, petrified yet transfixed.

None shall harm the tree.

It was Mole's voice. But he was not speaking, at least not with his mouth. The blue lips did not stir. She heard the voice speak a second time.

None shall harm the tree. None shall harm but *the tree. For those who come shall remain. And those who remain shall bear eternal witness to the power of the tree.*

Willow fell back and sat on the ground, hugging her knees to her chest. Mole's death had been no accident, of that she was sure. The tree had killed him. However ridiculous it might sound, she was convinced that it had strangled him with its roots. Her stomach churned and her mouth filled with acrid bile. She felt a hand on her shoulder. It was the policewoman.

"You've had an awful shock," she said. "Come away now."

As she spoke, she leant forward and placed her hand gently over Mole's face. When she removed it, the eyes were shut.

Finally, Mole looked to be at peace. If the words Willow had heard were true, however, there would be no peace for Mole's spirit – nor for any of the other victims of the tree.

Supported by the policewoman, Willow climbed shakily to her feet. Her body was weak. Her head spun.

None shall harm the tree.

None shall harm *but* the tree.

13

Kyle had remained outside the cordoned-off area when Willow suddenly dashed off to see Mole. He'd noticed the sudden change come over her when she was kneeling down next to the body and now, as the policewoman brought her back, he could see how deeply the experience had affected her. Her slim body looked oddly frail, her face pale and drawn.

"I'll leave her with you," the policewoman said, as she held up the plastic ribbon for Willow to go under. "She could do with a drink. Something sweet."

"Yeah. Thanks," said Kyle. "I'll see to that." He swung the knapsack down from his back, pulled a can of isotonic orange from inside and opened it. "Here," he said.

Willow took the drink and gulped it down thirstily.

"Better?" said Kyle.

Willow nodded wearily.

"What happened just then?" he asked.

Willow shrugged. "I ... I don't know. Something..." She paused. "Kyle," she said, "we've got to talk. But not here. Let's find somewhere quiet."

Kyle nodded. "That bad, eh?" he said.

Willow laughed humourlessly. "Worse," she said.

"Look," he said, as they walked away. "Whatever's going on here has got something to do with the history of the place. Agreed?"

Willow thought of the witch, the highwayman, the scruffy urchins. "Agreed," she said.

"So to understand what's gong on in the present," he went on, "we need to understand what happened in the past."

"You're right," said Willow. "Perhaps there'll be something in the town library. Old newspapers. Journals. Mind you," she said, looking at her watch, "it's probably shut by now. And tomorrow's Sunday."

Kyle laughed. "When you want to find something out you don't have to wait for the library to open any more," he said.

"What do you mean?" she said.

Before Kyle had a chance to explain, they both heard his name being called. "It's your mum," said Willow.

"Willow!" came a second voice.

"And yours," said Kyle.

They turned round to see Mrs Montcrieff and Sara, together with Blue, heading towards them.

"Have your heard the awful news?" said Sara. "About Mole."

Willow nodded.

"To die for a cause he believed in!" Mrs Montcrieff said. "I think he was so courageous. I think you all are," she said, looking from Willow to Sara. She turned to her son. "Don't you, Kyle?"

"Yes," he said, "Yes, I do." He looked at Willow. "In fact, we were just talking about what I could do, weren't we?" he said.

Willow nodded uncertainly.

"We thought it might be an idea to get on to the net and see what info there might be about the history of Marvis Ridge. Maybe set up a website."

Willow smiled and nodded knowingly, even though she hadn't the faintest idea what Kyle was talking about. She presumed it had something to do with computers. In Willow's life, her digital radio-alarm clock was about as high-tech as it went. If, however, she was right in thinking that Kyle was suggesting a way to check out the history of the place before Monday morning, then she was all for it.

"What exactly are you saying?" said Mrs Montcrieff, who was also completely ignorant about computers.

"We thought we'd look up the details of Marvis Ridge's past on the computer," Kyle spelt out.

"Excellent idea!" Mrs Montcrieff announced. "Who knows what you might uncover? Some old statute perhaps, that forbids the destruction of the trees. Or an obscure by-law that preserves ancient grazing rights..." She turned to Sara and beamed. "Never say die, my dear," she said. "Never say die."

Willow winced at the woman's choice of words. Kyle didn't seem to notice.

"The only problem," he was saying, "is how we get Willow back here later."

"Oh, she can stay the night," said Mrs Montcrieff brightly. "We've got stacks of room. And I take it we'll all be returning here tomorrow?" Kyle and Willow nodded. "That's settled then." She turned to Sara. "So long as it's all right with you."

"Willow's seventeen," Sara laughed. "It's up to her."

Although she had guessed that the Montcrieff family weren't short of a bob or two, Willow was taken aback by the grandeur of the White House. Tall and impressive, it stood at the end of a long, sweeping gravel drive, surrounded by poplars and copper beeches.

"The old place has been in the family for generations," Mrs Montcrieff explained. "In fact it was built by my great, great, great grandfather."

"It's amazing," said Willow.

"Far too big for the three of us, of course," she said, as she parked beside the front entrance. "And when Kyle's away, we rattle around in it like peas in a pod."

Willow smiled to herself and fought the temptation to talk about the plight of the homeless. She and Kyle followed Mrs Montcrieff inside. The hallway was floored with parquet tiles and the walls were lined with oak panels. It alone was at least three times the size of the bus that she, Sara, Gary and Blue travelled and lived in.

"Anyone for a cup of tea?" said Mrs Montcrieff.

"Not for me, thanks," said Willow.

"I think we'll get started at once," said Kyle, setting off up the stairs. Willow followed him. "I don't know how long it's all going to take."

"Good idea," Mrs Montcrieff nodded approvingly. She liked the interest Kyle was showing in the protest – even if, as she suspected, it had more to do with Willow's long legs and thick blonde hair than any sudden desire to save the Ridge. "I'll give you a shout when supper's ready," she said, but the pair had already gone.

Willow continued up the stairs with their thick pile carpet and ornately carved banisters. It was all so grand, so opulent! The tall Chinese porcelain vases on the half-landings. The intricate brass light fittings. The heavy gold framed portraits on the wall. It was like walking through a stately home or a museum, crammed with priceless works of art.

Kyle's room was right at the top of the house, directly under the roof. He unlocked the door and walked in. "Welcome to the Megabase," he said.

Willow stepped in and looked round her. "Wow!" she said. "It's incredible!"

"Like it?" said Kyle.

"Like it?" said Willow, as she looked round the massive room. "I love it."

The Megabase took up the whole of the top floor and was, unlike the rest of the house, full of high-tech, state-of-the-art gadgets and gizmos. In one corner was a long desk with a computer, printer and scanner, a fax machine and answer phone. Black speakers were fixed to the wall, and a stack-system music centre stood on its own tubular steel rack. Below it were rows of CDs, videos and computer discs. Above it, a wide-screen television.

And standing opposite the whole lot was a big, wide bed. Willow smiled.

The far end of the room had been turned into a work-out area complete with multi-gym, punch bag, bench and free weights. Beyond that was a door.

"What's through there?" asked Willow.

"The shower and loo," said Kyle. "There's a kettle in there, too," he added. "And a fridge. Fancy a lager?"

"Yeah," said Willow. "That would be nice."

As he disappeared, Willow once again found herself wondering what she was doing with Kyle Montcrieff, the boy who had everything. She knew she shouldn't like him at all. He was rich, pampered, posh. Yet for all that, she did like him – and fancied him. And after what they had been through together in the short time that they had known each other, Willow knew that she also trusted him.

When Kyle returned with the two misted bottles of ice-cold lager he found Willow sitting on his bed. "Here we are," he said, and handed her the bottle. "Cheers!"

They both swigged at the bottles.

"That hit the spot," said Kyle.

Willow looked up at him and smiled. She patted the bed beside her. "Why don't you sit down?" she said.

Kyle laughed. "I didn't bring you up here to look at my etchings," he said. "Honest!"

"I know you didn't," said Willow. "It's just. . ." Her eyes filled with water. "I need to talk."

Kyle sat down. He felt awkward. He felt excited. Willow traced her finger up and down the bottle. Drips of cold water dripped on to her jeans.

"About Mole?" he said.

Willow shrugged. "About everything," she said. Kyle put his beer down and slipped his arm around her. Willow didn't seem to notice. "I mean, if it was just the past I think I could handle it," she said. "You know, witches and highwaymen and that, but this... This is the present. This is now! Oh Kyle," she said, "I'm so frightened."

Kyle drew her towards him and hugged her tightly. She was so beautiful. "It'll be all right," he whispered. "You'll see."

Willow looked up. She liked the feel of his arms around her, the look of concern in his eyes, the way his mouth puckered up when he whispered *you'll*. She reached up and kissed him softly. Then again. She ran her fingers through his thick hair. She pulled him closer.

Kyle could hardly believe his luck. He pushed aside all thoughts that he was taking advantage of her distress over Mole's death. It wasn't true anyway. They had kissed before – before they were so hideously interrupted by the tree. He leaned backwards, pulling Willow down on to the bed with him and kissed her some more. On her burning cheeks, on her pointy nose, on her soft, full lips – feeling her kissing him back.

He rolled over on top of her. She wrapped her arms around his neck and stared up into his eyes. She smiled back and pulled him towards her...

"Waaaah!" Kyle exclaimed, and leapt up.

Willow looked at the frothing bottle in her hand and burst out laughing. "Whoops!" she said.

Kyle pulled his sweatshirt off and daubed at the bed and the back of his neck. "It's freezing!" he said.

"Just come out of the fridge, hasn't it?" said Willow, and laughed again. "Come on," she said. "I think it's time we got down to the matter in hand."

"I thought we had," said Kyle, with a grin.

Willow groaned. "You know what I mean." She smiled. "There'll be time for any other business later on."

"All right then," said Kyle reluctantly as he climbed off the bed. He walked over to the computer and switched it on. "Let's see what we can find. Pull up a chair."

The pair of them sat down at the desk, and Kyle set the computer running. Willow could only watch as he manoeuvred the mouse this way and that, clicking and double-clicking, as a series of pictures, diagrams and icons came up on the screen. She hadn't a clue what he was doing, but it all looked very clever.

Finally, he turned and looked at her. "Right," he said. "What do you think we should start with? How about Marvis Ridge?"

"OK," said Willow.

Kyle typed in the command.

Nothing found.

"Well, that's a good start," Willow snorted.

"Hey," Kyle laughed. "Don't be so impatient."

He leant forwards and patted the computer affectionately. "Window to the world," he said. "All the information we need is in there somewhere. It's just a matter of pinning it down."

"The Tourist Board," said Willow.

"You what?" said Kyle.

"Bridgemorton Tourist Board," said Willow. "They'll have stuff on the Ridge. Do you think they'd be in the net?"

Kyle laughed. "*On* the net," he said. "Yeah, bound to be. Everyone's on the net these days."

He typed and clicked. *Searching*, announced the screen, and a list of possibles appeared. More typing and clicking. More *searching*. "We're homing in," said Kyle, as he typed and clicked still more. All at once, a page of text emerged. Kyle scrolled down until he came to a sub-heading: *The History of Marvis Ridge*. "Yeah!" he said, and punched the air. "We're off!"

The information was scanty. There was mention of a neolithic settlement, an old priory, a battle between Roundheads and Cavaliers. Not much, but enough to lead them on. They decided to make their own list of all the possible headings they could check under.

Tom Marley

Mayor Fothergill

Witchcraft

Lizzie (?)

The Battle of Marvis Ridge
Local legends
St Marbell's Priory...

Then they made a second list of all the places where they might find the information: newspaper archives, parish records, books and magazines... And when that was finished, they began, slowly and systematically, to assemble all the information they could find.

By the time Mrs Montcrieff called them for supper, they had established two important facts: one, that at least some of the phantoms they had seen were historical figures. And two, that the deadly influence of the tree itself had been mooted many centuries earlier.

Tom Marley (1709–1738), for instance, was apparently a notorious highwayman who had been hanged behind Marvis Ridge on April 27. As he died he was reported to have cried out, "This tree be damned." There was an artist's impression of the man, though the picture of the shifty-eyed, snarling-mouthed highwayman bore scant resemblance to the person Willow had seen.

Mayor Fothergill (1681–1739) was also mentioned. He had died at the selfsame spot a year after Marley's hanging, when his horse had fatally unseated him.

And the witch – the Lizzie of Kyle's recurring nightmares – proved also to be a real person. In 1572, one Elizabeth Greatorex was executed for witchcraft. The manner of her death was particularly gruesome. She was covered in pitch, suspended from the bough of "a great oake", and burned alive. Kyle and Willow shuddered. There was no doubt as to which oak was being referred to in the ancient text.

"Kyle! Willow!" Mrs Montcrieff called for a second time. "Your supper's on the table."

"Coming," Kyle called back. They read on.

As her bodye did blaze like to a flaming torch, so did incantations issue from her wicked lips.

> *"I curse again this 'cursed Tree,*
> *Whose* viscum album *tempted Me,*
> *Whose Evilnesse hath seized my very Soul...*

Willow turned and stared at Kyle. "Cursed," she said. "Over four hundred years ago."

"Before that, by the sound of it," said Kyle. He frowned "What's *viscum album*?"

"Mistletoe," said Willow. "No self-respecting witch would ever be without it. It's been known for its magical powers for thousands of years," she went on, happy to have something to tell him for a change. "From Druids to homoeopaths. Of course, during the witchhunts, being caught collecting the stuff would have been dangerous – particularly if you had a warty nose."

"Kyle! Willow!" shouted Mrs Montcrieff. "Your supper's getting cold. Will you please come down now!"

"Coming!" Kyle shouted back. "We'd better go," he said, jumping up from his chair. "Anyway, I've hardly eaten all day. I'm starving."

Willow nodded, but returned to the verse on the screen. She couldn't wait till after dinner to read the end. As the words sank in, her heart began to pound. They referred not only to Lizzie Greatorex herself, but to everyone else who might stumble upon the tree for ever after: Thomas Marley, the naughty boys, Mole, perhaps even herself. "Listen to this," she said.

> *For those who come shall ever stay,*
> *Saints and Sinners likewyse shall pay.*
> *The Tree of Death, and the Lives it stole –*
> *So long it stands, so shall the Death-Knell toll.*

14

The Tree of Death! Willow supposed that in one respect, it was a relief to discover that the oak tree was indeed haunted. At least it confirmed that she wasn't going mad. But the Tree of Death! What could be more insane than the existence of a tree which – if Lizzie Greatorex was to be believed – was so evil that it attracted death and suffering to itself in order to steal its victims' souls? As she followed Kyle down to the dining-room, Willow felt her appetite ebb away.

The meal was delicious – pasta with a spicy sauce of tomatoes, garlic, olives, capers, anchovies and tuna, topped with parmesan. But Willow could only pick. The ominous words of the verse had frightened her, and her stomach felt as if it had shrunk to the size of a knotted fist.

Not so Kyle. He shovelled the food in, three helpings in all. Willow had never seen anyone eat so much. What was more, when the dishes had been cleared away, she discovered to her horror that the pasta dish was just the starter.

"I couldn't," she said, as Mrs Montcrieff returned to the dining room bearing a bowl of salad and two plates, each covered with an enormous slab of medium-rare steak. "I just couldn't," she said. "I ... I..."

Mrs Montcrieff laughed. "It's all right, dear," she said. "I'm sure it won't go to waste."

They both looked at Kyle, who nodded, swallowed and smiled back at them. "Just pass it over here," he said, patting his stomach fondly. "Plenty of room inside."

Mrs Montcrieff chuckled to herself as she left the room. Willow shook her head in disbelief.

"Doesn't it bother you?" she said. "Everything that's been happening."

"Bother me?" Kyle mumbled. "Of course it bothers me. It's absolutely terrifying." He looked up. "But I can't think straight on an empty stomach."

"*For those who come shall ever stay*," said Willow thoughtfully. "Do you think that means you and me?"

"Might," said Kyle, sawing off another chunk of meat with his steak knife. "Might not. It hasn't done us any real harm so far, has it?"

"And what about Blue? And Gary?" Willow continued. "He was planning on sleeping up in the tree tonight. He could be in real danger. I *knew* I shouldn't have left them all."

Kyle paused, his forkful poised by his lips. "If you hadn't left them you'd never have discovered how much danger they were in," he said logically. "Anyway, all we've done is to confirm what we already knew before. What we need to discover now is why the tree was cursed in the first place."

Willow was uncertain. "And then what?" she said. "We know what the tree is capable of when it senses danger. Look what happened to us." She paused. "And you know what? The more I think of it, the more convinced I am that it strangled Mole. There were bits of root around his neck."

"Strangled him?" Kyle spluttered. "Even if it were possible, he wasn't anywhere near it."

"A tree that size?" said Willow. "The roots must go on for ever. I'll bet any money Mole had started to dig into the root system and..." She stopped, suddenly overcome with a vision of her friend's frantic attempts to release the tightening around his neck, of his gasping mouth, of the terror in his eyes. Underground. In the darkness. *Oh, Mole!* she thought. *You must have been so frightened.*

"We'll look it up," said Kyle, trying to sound matter-of-fact. "Check just how far the roots can spread." He shrugged. "In normal trees, I don't think they go further than the canopy overhead."

"The Tree of Death is not a normal tree," she snapped.

"But—"

"Listen, Kyle," she said, "I've been working it out. Pooh Bear Tunnel was a bit over a hundred metres long, right? The distance across that flowery woodland between the camp and the edge of the darker forest. That was how far he'd got." She sniffed. "Too far," she added. "Too close to the Tree of Death."

"I don't understand," said Kyle.

"Do you remember smelling garlic this morning?" she said. "Just as we came to the top of the slope."

"Yes," said Kyle slowly. "Yes, I do. But what of it?"

Willow told him all about the rhyme that Blue had learnt from the two boys, Eddy and Jack. *Ring of garlic! Garlic ring! It keeps the evil out! It keeps the evil in!* The exact meaning had been bothering her ever since she had first heard it.

"And you think—" he said.

"I think that the ring is the outer extent of the oak tree's roots, radiating out in all directions. Everything within that ring, above and below, is ... is,

I don't know ... *influenced* by the tree. Under its control."

"But it says it keeps the evil out, too," said Kyle.

Willow shrugged. "Perhaps that means anything which might harm the tree," she suggested.

"Or perhaps not," said Kyle, meaningfully. "Come on. I'll skip pud. Let's get back upstairs. There's a few things we need to add to that list of ours."

They were up on the first-floor landing when the front door slammed. Willow jumped. Kyle put his finger to his lips.

"It's Father," he whispered.

"Hello, dear," they heard Mrs Montcrieff saying. "Good game of golf?"

"I won, if that's what you mean," he snapped.

Mrs Montcrieff fell silent, waiting for an explanation for his awful mood. It wasn't long in coming.

"It's taken me three hours to get back!" he exploded. "Three hours! Bloody road blocks because of the bloody protests up at Marvis Ridge. Bloody riff-raff."

"Never mind, dear," she said. "You're here now. And I've kept your dinner warm."

"I haven't got time for dinner," he said. "There's a Lodge meeting at eight."

"So there is," said Mrs Montcrieff. "I'd forgotten."

"Father's a Freemason," Kyle said in explanation.

That figures! thought Willow.

"I could make you a sandwich," Mrs Montcrieff offered. "Ham? Cheese and pickle?"

Mr Montcrieff ignored her. "Rod told me the eviction papers were served this afternoon, giving them till Thursday to go," he went on. "Get shot of the bloody layabouts once and for all."

"Rodney Bickley," whispered Kyle. "Father's golf partner. He's the Under Sheriff of Bridgemorton."

Willow nodded.

"Anyway," Mr Montcrieff went on, "since that young idiot got himself killed, everything's been brought forward. They're moving in on Monday. An assault from the south, bright and early." He laughed unpleasantly. "While the tribe of great unwashed are still asleep."

"Not now they won't be," said Willow softly.

"Somebody died, then?" said Mrs Montcrieff. "How dreadful."

"They've got no right," Mr Montcrieff grumbled. "I mean I've got nothing against them endangering their own lives – all for it, in fact – but what about all the others? The guards, the police, the rescue teams, all risking their lives for the sake of these parasites, these oiks—"

"Yes, dear," said Mrs Montcieff calmly. "Now, would you like that sandwich or not?"

"No," he said. "I haven't got time. I'm going up to get showered and changed."

At the sound of his father's heavy footsteps on the staircase, Kyle pulled Willow away. The pair of them disappeared up the next flight of stairs and took refuge in the Megabase. Kyle shut the door silently behind him.

"They're not very alike, your parents," Willow commented.

"They used to be," said Kyle. He shrugged. "Or maybe they weren't. I never knew Mother was such a good actress. Come on, then. Let's get back to work."

It wasn't long before the pair of them were once more totally engrossed in the task at hand. After a slow start, they had a sudden breakthrough when Kyle came across the newspaper library's cross-filing index. Suddenly *Marvis Ridge* yielded all kinds of relevant articles. The information came thick and fast. It was a catalogue of disasters.

In 1801, two charcoal burners had been found hacked to death with each other's axes "beneath a great oak". In 1534, a shepherd boy called Dan had somehow hanged himself up an oak tree while taking refuge from a wild boar, while in 1742, Lady Amelia Fitzroy-Hooper had died instantly when her bolting horse had galloped beneath "a spreading oak tree" and she had struck her head against a low branch.

From the bottom of the house came the sound of the front door slamming. Kyle raised his eyebrows to heaven. "There he goes," he said. "Off to the Brownies."

Willow laughed. "What do masons actually do?" she said.

"Dunno," said Kyle. "But they need an apron and a trowel to do it." He squinted at the screen. "Now *that's* interesting," he said.

"What?" said Willow.

Without answering, Kyle moved the mouse this way and that, clicked, double-clicked and typed in a series of commands. Suddenly, the screen filled with a chronological list of occurrences of freak weather conditions on the Ridge. A hurricane, two whirlwinds, blizzards, two weeks of impenetrable fog, thunderstorms, hailstones and flooding – and all of them resulting in further deaths at or around the fateful oak tree. "There!" he announced.

Willow leant forward, squinted at the screen – and there it was. During a particularly violent storm in 1888, a lightning bolt had struck a branch of the tree, causing the deaths of two boys who were climbing it at the time.

"Edward and John Faulkner," she read out. "Eddy and Jack. The two naughty boys." She turned to Kyle. "That blackened scar on the side of the trunk," she said. "It must have been where the lightning struck."

Kyle nodded. "And the boys fell and were crushed."

"Oh, it's all so horrible," said Willow. "All those people who died – victims of the Tree of Death. How many have there been?"

Kyle checked down his list. "Including the Faulkner brothers, seventeen," he said, "so far."

"And the trouble is," Willow said, "seen individually, they all look like accidents. It's only when you put them together that it starts to look suspicious."

"I know," said Kyle. "Everything brings us back to the oak tree. What was it Lizzie Greatorex said? *I curse again this 'cursed Tree*. We still haven't found out why it was already cursed."

Willow yawned. "The oldest reference we've got of the area is the monastery—"

"The *priory*," Kyle corrected her. "St Marbell's. I know. And since both you and Gary saw hooded figures who could have been monks, I'm sure it'd help to find out more about it. The problem is how. I can't find anything about it. Nothing at all."

Not that he was about to give up and, as the hour grew late and Willow more and more sleepy, Kyle tried everything he could think of to access more information on the elusive St Marbell's Priory. When, at eleven o'clock, his latest attempt also came to nothing, Willow sighed.

"It's no use," she said. "I've got to get some sleep."

"Yeah?" said Kyle. "I think I'll keep searching." He turned. "Do you... Shall I show you the spare room?"

Willow smiled and gave him a kiss. "No," she said. "I'll just lie down here if that's all right. But if you find anything, I want you to wake me at once."

"Course I will," said Kyle.

Willow stood up, yawned again, dragged herself over to Kyle's bed and lay down. The bed was soft but firm. Much more comfortable than anything she'd slept on since that last visit to her grandma's. That reminded her – before she left Kyle's house, she wanted to have a bath. A long, hot ... steaming ... scented bath...

Kyle smiled to himself as the soft, rhythmic sound of sleepy breathing filled the air. He turned and looked at her, curled up on his bed, her long fair hair splayed across his pillow, her delicate fists clenched. She'd been through so much: the nightmare – if that was what it had been – of Tom Marley's hanging, the awful visions he and she shared on the platform of the tree, the death of her friend Mole.

He walked over to the bed and pulled the duvet up around her. "I'll find out why it happened," he whispered, and kissed her on the cheek. "I promise I will."

Back at the computer, Kyle took a swig of beer, scratched his head and returned to the screen with renewed determination.

"St Marbell's," he muttered. "St Marbell's. Where are you hiding, damn you!"

15

Bright sun and birdsong woke Willow. She rolled over and looked round. She was in the Megabase, she remembered, on Kyle's bed. She glanced at her watch. It was just gone half-past six.

Kyle, she realized with a twinge of regret, hadn't come to bed at all. She sat up on her elbows and looked across the room at him. Although he was still sitting at the desk, his head was resting on his arms and he was snoring gently. The screen – on energy saver – was displaying a never-ending looped doodle which changed through the colours of the rainbow as it slowly twisted round and round.

Willow sighed with disappointment. Since he'd promised to wake her if he found anything, it could mean only one thing: he'd drawn a blank.

She sat up, hugged her legs to her chest and watched him. One thing was for certain: he would have tried his best. Just then he stirred, and his head shifted round from one side to the other and settled. The rhythmic rising and falling of his huge shoulders continued.

Willow recalled how good it had felt having his arms wrapped around her. They had reassured her, they had made her feel safe. She wanted a hug now. She wanted a kiss. She wanted lots of kisses.

Kyle stirred again. This time he was awake. He sat up, looked round and smiled dreamily at her.

"I knew you were looking at me," he said. "I could feel it."

"I was not," said Willow hotly. "Arrogant pig! I only looked up when you looked round."

"What were you doing then?" he asked.

"Meditating, if you must know," she lied, and quickly changed the subject. "I take it you didn't find anything out."

"Oh, I found loads of stuff," he said. "For a start, the body count's up to thirty-eight."

"But you said you'd wake me," Willow protested.

"I know, but—" He winced. "Hang on," he said. "Let me just brush my teeth. My mouth tastes as though something's died in it."

As he disappeared into the bathroom, Willow jumped off the bed. The screen continued with its display of wiggly lines. She stared at it helplessly, wishing once again that she knew more about computers. She grabbed hold of the mouse, as she'd seen Kyle do. Immediately, the screen filled with text. She looked at the heading: *The Priorie of Marvels*.

"I found it by a process of elimination," Kyle explained as he returned from the bathroom. He sat down beside her. Willow could smell toothpaste on his breath as he told her how the Bridgemorton Tourist Board – from whom they had first learned of the priory – had misspelt the name.

"So it's got nothing to do with the *bells*," she said. "Marbell. I thought—"

"So did I," said Kyle. "And he wasn't a saint either. That's why I couldn't find it in the Church Register."

"Well, I think you were really clever to get the right name," said Willow.

Kyle looked down sheepishly, and scratched behind his ear. "Actually, it was a complete fluke," he admitted. "A typing error. B and V are next to each other on the keyboard."

Willow burst out laughing and thumped him on the arm. "Process of elimination!" she said scornfully. "You old fraud."

"Came up with the right result though, didn't I?" said Kyle.

"Yes," said Willow. "Yes, you did. And well done."

"The thing is, it suddenly all makes sense. Marbell. Marvell. Marvels. Marvis. The Ridge itself is named after the priory."

Willow nodded excitedly. "So what exactly have you found out about it?"

"Not that much," said Kyle. "It was founded in 1212 and destroyed in 1313. As for the hundred and one years in between, there's precious little."

"And nothing about the oak tree?"

"Nothing."

"This is completely hopeless," said Willow. "We're no better off than before."

"Aren't we?" said Kyle. "I'm not so sure. I keep coming back to that last line of Lizzie Greatorex's verse: *So long it stands, so shall the Death Knell toll.*" He looked round at Willow. "Do you understand?" he said. "If the killing is to be stopped then the tree must be destroyed."

Willow remained silent. Of course she understood, but having spent half her life trying to prevent valleys being flooded, marshes being drained, meadows being tarmacked and trees being felled, how could she now advocate the destruction of the most magnificent oak tree she had ever seen?

"Why can't we just leave it?" she said. "It's in such a secluded spot and—"

"Thirty-eight deaths," Kyle reminded her. "The last one yesterday."

Willow's head spun. She knew in her heart that

he was right. But she knew also that if Sara, Gary or any of the others found out what was being proposed, she would be treated like a traitor, a pariah – she would no longer be welcome to travel with them. Then again, if the evil tree remained standing, how many more victims might it claim?

"Even if I agreed," she said finally, "how would we go about it? The tree's impregnable."

Kyle nodded. "I've been thinking about that," he said. "Father said that the bailiffs were going to come from the south, didn't he? Up the front of the ridge, before the final date on the eviction notice and catching everyone unawares."

"Yes," said Willow. "We've got to get back and warn them."

"Which means," Kyle went on, "that they'll come to the oak tree last, once everything else has been felled. Now, if they came from the north instead, then everything would be reversed. The oak tree would be one of the first trees to go – which is what we want. What's more, the noise would alert the others so that they could take up their positions and defend the rest of Marvis Ridge properly."

Willow listened thoughtfully. "Two birds with one stone," she said. "But how do we get them to change from south to north? They must have—"

"My father," Kyle interrupted. "If we pitch it to him right, he'll make sure old Rodders the Under Sheriff gets to hear of it."

"And how *do* we pitch it to him?" asked Willow. "I mean, it doesn't make any sense for them to come from the north for all the reasons you've given."

Kyle smiled. "Leave it to me," he said.

Mr Montcrieff had already finished his breakfast when Kyle entered the dining room. He looked up from his newspaper. "Morning," he said. "It's not like you to be down for breakfast so early. I..." He caught sight of Willow. "Hello?" he said.

"Good morning, Mr Montcrieff," said Willow.

"Willow's a friend of mine," said Kyle. "She stayed the night."

Mr Montcrieff pulled himself out of his chair and leant across the table, hand outstretched. "Pleased to meet you," he said.

Willow shook his hand shyly. Kyle's father was nothing like how she had imagined him from the deep, angry voice she had heard the previous evening. He was considerably shorter than Kyle, and wiry. His face was ashen and drawn, his hair greying and thin, and he had small dark eyes which darted round constantly as he spoke. "So," he said to Willow. "I take it you're not from Travers?"

"No," said Willow. "I live ... locally."

Mr Montcrieff nodded. "And you met Kyle..."

"At the swimming baths," Kyle butted in. He didn't want his father to know that Willow had anything to do with the "bloody riff-raff" up on Marvis Ridge.

Mr Montcrieff nodded again. "Do you play tennis?" he said.

"Not that well," Willow admitted.

"Why do you ask?" said Kyle.

"I'm going up to the club later," his father said. "Having a game with Rod. We could make it doubles if you like."

"We'll take a rain check on that one, thanks," said Kyle.

Confused, Mr Montcrieff stared at him. "Another one of your horrible Americanisms, eh? Does it mean yes or no?"

Kyle laughed. "No," he said. "At least, not today. We're planning on going for a long walk."

"Well, the offer's there if you change your mind," he said, and returned to his newspaper. As he flipped it round, Kyle and Willow found themselves staring at the headline of the article he had just finished reading: *Tunnel Tragedy for Bypass Protester*. They glanced at one another. Kyle spoke.

"What's that about a tunnel tragedy?" he asked innocently. "Is it anything to do with the protest up on the Ridge?"

Mr Montcrieff looked over his paper. "It is," he said. "Some young idiot..." He turned back to the article. "Andrew 'Mole' Butterworth. He died underground." He shook his head. "I really don't know what these people hope to achieve."

"I think they're hoping to prevent the destruction of Marvis Ridge," said Willow. She smiled. "An area of outstanding natural beauty."

Mr Montcrieff looked up at her suspiciously. "Are they now?" he said. "And I suppose you agree with what they're doing?"

"No one wants the Ridge destroyed," said Kyle.

"But everyone wants the traffic in town reduced," said Mr Montcrieff, and shrugged, as though that were an end to the matter.

Kyle scratched his head. "I thought there were plans for a tunnel," he said.

Mr Montcrieff snorted. "Eight hundred million pounds, the bypass will cost if they cut through the Ridge. If they build a tunnel it'll cost nearly two billion. Two *billion*!"

"Is that an American or a British billion?" asked Willow.

"I beg your pardon? said Mr Montrieff.

"You see, an American billion is a thousand million," she explained. "A British billion is a million million." She turned to Kyle. "It's funny how the two are used. On the news, the other night, the government announced that the proposed Treddethel Nuclear Power Station would cost five thousand million pounds to build. A snip! Yet on the same news, foreign aid was given as one and a half *billion* pounds. American billions, of course, but in our heads we think of the British ones." She turned to Mr Montcrieff and smiled sweetly. "I know just what you mean about horrible Americanisms."

Mr Montcrieff shuffled his paper around awkwardly, not quite sure how to take her comments. Kyle, for his part, had seldom seen his father looking so flustered – it was all he could do to keep a straight face.

"All I know is this," said Mr Montcrieff finally. "We need the bypass, and a tunnel would be prohibitively expensive."

Willow held her tongue. There were some people you simply couldn't argue with.

"So I expect they'll be moving them on, then?" said Kyle. "The protesters, I mean."

"They certainly will," said Mr Montcrieff, relieved that the conversation had returned to something he knew more about. He chuckled. "And sooner than they think."

"Of course it won't be easy," said Kyle thoughtfully. "I saw on the news that they keep a permanent look-out. And there's such an excellent view from the top, they'd spot anyone coming a mile off – if they came from the south, that is."

"Oh, I doubt whether they'd be that stupid," Willow joined in. "There's that little B-road just north of the Ridge, isn't there? They'll probably go that way. The woods are so thick there, they wouldn't be seen."

"Until it was too late," added Kyle. "Though it can be a bit swampy."

"With this drought?" said Willow. "It'll be dry as a bone."

Mr Montcrieff, who had been following their conversation with interest, turned to Kyle. "I believe there might have been concerns about getting the heavy vehicles through the trees that way," he said.

"Oh, there's no problem on that score," said Kyle. "The whole area's criss-crossed with bridleways."

"I see," said Mr Montcrieff, and shrugged. "I daresay there were other considerations." He folded up his paper and tucked it under his arm. "You sure you won't join me for tennis?" he said.

"Positive," said Kyle.

"Perhaps another time," said Willow.

"Careful!" said Kyle. "He'll hold you to that."

Mr Montcrieff laughed. "Enjoy your walk," he said.

As the door clicked shut behind him, Willow turned to Kyle, and the pair of them broke into stifled laughter.

"You were fantastic!" said Kyle. "And all that stuff about *billions*. I don't know how I stopped myself from laughing."

"You weren't too bad yourself," Willow laughed. "Do you think he swallowed it?"

"Hook, line and sinker," said Kyle. "An hour from now and the Under Sheriff of Bridgemorton will know everything there is to know about the advantages of moving in from the north."

"Let's just hope he listens," said Willow.

Kyle laughed. "My father is a very persuasive man."

Just then the door opened. Kyle and Willow spun round guiltily. Had he heard what they'd been saying?

Mrs Montcrieff appeared in the doorway, and started back. "Ooh, you gave me a fright! I had no idea you were down already. Sleep well, did you, Willow? Good. Now, what would you like for breakfast, dear?"

"Just some toast and coffee, please," she said.

"And the usual for you, Kyle?"

Kyle nodded. "With extra sausages, please," he said, and looked at Willow. "We've got a long day in front of us."

16

Breakfast took longer than Willow had thought it would. While she nibbled at her slice of toast and honey and sipped her black coffee Kyle demolished his "usual" – three bananas, four Shredded Wheat, and a massive fry-up.

"I've never seen anyone eat so much!" she complained.

Kyle grinned. "Got to keep my strength up. I'm due a workout in the gym later on," he said and, clasping his arms above his head, stretched his shoulders round first one way, then the other. "I get all tensed up if I miss a session."

"Well, I'm going up to the Ridge with your mum straight after breakfast," said Willow sharply.

"Maybe I'll see you up there later, then," said

Kyle. Willow stared at him in furious disbelief. "Only joking!" Kyle laughed, raising his hands defensively.

"You'd better be!" said Willow. "And I don't want you leaving me while we're up there, all right! Not for an instant."

"How could I resist an offer like that?" Kyle grinned.

"I'm serious," said Willow. "I do not intend to be number thirty-nine on the tree's hit list."

Kyle looked at her. There was fear in those green eyes of hers, and her hands were shaking. He leant forward and took hold of her fingers. "You're right," he said. "I shouldn't be making light of this." He smiled. "We're going to be just fine."

Willow smiled. "That's what they said in that film *Lava* – just before the volcano erupted!"

With Kyle's plate finally empty, and all the breakfast things whisked away to the dishwasher, they were ready to leave. As Willow followed the other two out through the front door, she sighed with a mixture of sadness and resignation. She loved sleeping under a roof so much. Now, returning to her tent, she felt like she did whenever she left Grandma's house – only more so.

"You must come and visit again," said Mrs Montcrieff, as if reading her mind.

"Thanks," said Willow. "I'd like that." She climbed into the back of the Range Rover, and looked back longingly at the White House as they set off down the driveway. And next time, she vowed, she would have that bath she'd been dreaming of, rather than just a shower.

They drove back through the beige and khaki landscape in silence, each one wondering when – or whether – it would ever rain again. At Frog Corner Mrs Montcrieff turned to Kyle.

"I've made a decision," she said.

"What?" he said.

"I've decided to tell them."

Kyle frowned. "Who?" he said.

"The protesters," she said. "Your father told me something last night that I don't feel I can keep to myself." Both Kyle and Willow guessed what she was talking about, but let her continue. "They received eviction notices last night," she said. "They've been told to go by Thursday. But the authorities are planning on going in on Monday morning. And I don't think that's right," she said hotly. "So I'm going to tell the protesters everything I know."

Kyle glanced round at Willow. If she did tell them, it could ruin everything. The protesters would be up all night, waiting for any sign of the bailiffs and bulldozers – even from the north. If that happened, the evil tree would never be destroyed. And that, as they both now believed, was of paramount importance.

"Perhaps that's not such a good idea," said Willow.

"Why on earth not?" said Mrs Montcrieff, swerving slightly with surprise.

"I know them," said Willow. "They'll stay up all night waiting. Drinking. Smoking. They won't be fit for anything by the time the bulldozers actually do arrive."

Mrs Montcrieff shook her head uncertainly. "But surely, forewarned is forarmed," she said.

"I promise you," said Willow. "If they arrive out of the blue on Monday they'll face far more opposition than if they leave it till the Thursday deadline."

"You can see Willow's point," said Kyle. "Much better that they've all had a good night's sleep."

Mrs Montcrieff breathed in sharply. "All right," she said. "If you're sure, I'll take your word for it. But I hope, for the sake of Marvis Ridge, that you're right."

So do I, thought Willow. *So do I*.

As they approached the Ridge, Mrs Montcrieff rounded the final corner – and immediately had to slam her brakes on to avoid running into the stationary car in front. The news of Mole's death had attracted yet more people from all round – a mixture of the ghoulish and the concerned – and a column of vehicles was inching its way along the road, up the track and into the makeshift car-park in the upper fields.

"We're going to be stuck here for some while," said Mrs Montcrieff. "Why don't you two jump out? I'll catch up with you in the camp."

Neither Kyle nor Willow needed telling twice. They'd both been wondering how they would split up from Kyle's mother painlessly. Now they had the perfect opportunity. They jumped out, hurried past the line of cars and vans, and on up towards Camp Didgeridoo.

The place was thronging, yet the atmosphere was hushed. Mole's death and the subsequent serving of the eviction notices had left everyone involved feeling anxious and subdued, uncertain what to do for the best. Pausing only briefly to ask Ally whether she had seen Sara or Gary that morning (which she hadn't), Kyle and Willow continued past the tents and benders, and up into the woodland beyond.

And as they walked, so they talked. About schoolfriends and exams, about music and films, about life in a boarding school and life on board a bus. Willow told Kyle all about her old pet guinea pig, Arthur, and about Mrs Arneson – and her real dad. And Kyle talked of the rugby cups he'd helped win for the school, and the boxing trophies he'd won for himself. They talked about everything, that is, except the tree.

Yet with every reluctant step, they were getting nearer. There was no doubt about that. Their hearts were thumping. Their heads were spinning. Neither of them wanted to see the tree ever again, yet they had to satisfy themselves that the trucks and bulldozers would be able to reach the oak tree from the north. If not, then all their efforts to change the Under Sheriff's plans would have been for nothing. By the time they came to the ring of garlic, both Kyle and Willow were shuddering with the forbidding chill that emanated from the cursed tree.

"Let's just follow the ring round," said Willow.

"OK," said Kyle. Anything that meant putting off going into the tree's circle of influence sounded good to him. They headed round to the west, guided as much by their noses as their eyes, with the wild garlic steaming in the stifling heat. After a while, they came to a narrow clearing.

"This is the bridleway that leads to where we're camped," she said.

Kyle nodded. The ring of garlic curved round towards the north-east. The pair of them kept walking. To their left, the woods thinned. To their right, the trees grew thicker than ever.

"Father was right," Kyle commented. "You could barely get through here with a bicycle, let alone a bulldozer."

Willow said nothing. The ring curved round to

161

the east. Suddenly, in front of them, they heard the sound of a single car. The next moment, they emerged on the narrow road. The ring of garlic continued along the verge.

They walked along the sticky tarmac in silence. To the north, now, were fields of golden corn. To the south, the forest continued, dense, dark and deep. They were on the point of giving up hope of finding any easy way in when Willow caught sight of a sign up ahead. On it was a single word, white on green.

"Bridleway," she read.

Kyle grinned. "Told you," he said.

"I never doubted you for a moment," said Willow.

"Liar," laughed Kyle.

As they got closer, they could see that this second bridleway offered the perfect access to the protesters' camps. Two stone posts – gateless and skewiff – marked the beginning of the track. Bracken grew there, and rosebay willow-herb, but nothing that would impede the progress of the heavy vehicles. In fact as far as Willow could tell, apart from the one tall tree, the ancient bridleway cut a swathe right through from where they were standing to Crow's Nest Camp itself.

She stood staring at the tree. It was tall, it was imposing, it dwarfed everything else nearby – the Tree of Death.

"You don't think they'll just go round it, do you?" said Willow.

Kyle shrugged. "They'll probably send some of the vehicles round. But remember, this is an eviction. If someone's up on Gary's platform, then they'll stop to take them off. And it's the occupied trees they're planning on demolishing first."

Willow nodded uncertainly, and shuddered. Now that she had learnt so much about the evil tree, the thought of anyone having to climb up again into its branches filled her with clammy dread.

She stared ahead, transfixed by the leaves that sparkled like water in the sunlight, and sighed. What could possibly have happened in the dim, distant past to make the tree so wicked? Who had laid that first curse? Unknown to her, Kyle was wondering the selfsame things – all those questions they had avoided on their way there. Like her, although he'd managed not to talk about the tree, he hadn't been able to stop thinking about it. How was it possible that something so beautiful could ever have become so evil?

Still lost in their thoughts, neither Willow nor Kyle noticed the minute changes taking place around them as they walked. They didn't see the sky darken, nor the undergrowth retreat, nor the bracken close its fingered leaves and spiral away to nothing.

They passed through the ancient gateposts. The

air shimmered. They crossed the ring. The odour of crushed garlic filled their nostrils, the sound of whispering voices filled their ears. *It keeps the evil in. It keeps the evil out.*

Willow trembled and reached out for Kyle's hand. She knew now that they had made a mistake in leaving the safety of the road. Yet the tree was too strong for her – for them both. Even as their heads told them to turn and run, their bodies, like the bodies of mindless automatons, continued walking towards the mesmerizing tree.

The sky turned acrid yellow. The whispers became screams.

"No!" Willow cried out. "We've got to get away." She turned and began running back the way they had come, still clutching Kyle's hand.

Faster and faster they raced, yet no matter how far they went, nor how quickly they ran, the gateposts remained elusively out of reach. In fact, instead of coming nearer, they seemed almost to be receding farther into the distance. It was as though Willow and Kyle were travelling the wrong way along a moving pavement.

Finally – breathless and scared half to death – Willow stopped. She turned to face Kyle. "There's no ... no way out," she panted. "No escape."

All round them the air sparkled and danced. An unnatural hush descended. Both Willow and Kyle sensed something at their shoulders.

Slowly, tentatively, they turned their heads.

Kyle groaned, Willow gave a squeak of surprise. All their running had been in vain, for there, directly behind them and draped in a swirling, sulphurous mist, was the tree. The Tree of Death.

A sour breeze blew, thinning the mist and sending it dancing off in flimsy wisps. They stared at the tree, crestfallen and dumbfounded.

"But—" said Willow.

"I don't understand," said Kyle.

The mist continued to thin, and the glittering ceased. There was no doubt. The tree, which had once stood more than forty metres high, was now lying on its side.

For a moment Kyle and Willow thought they must be catching a glimpse of a future where the tree had been uprooted and defeated – but only for a moment. This tree was smaller than the one they had climbed. Suddenly they were both struck by the fearful realization that this was not the future they were seeing, but the past.

What was more, they were not alone.

17

Although they were still standing in the gloomy forest, everything had subtly changed. It was as though the trees themselves had been shuffling about under cover of the mist. Now the mist had gone, nothing was quite as it had been before.

Too terrified to move, Kyle and Willow stood stockstill, taking the situation in. They were surrounded by a circle of monks – a hundred or so – all dressed in long, dark robes and heavy cowls, whose deep melancholy voices echoed through the trees beyond the clearing as they sang their haunting mass.

Morning was close, but each one was holding aloft a scented, flaming torch. Together, they cast a golden glow upon the ground and filled the air with the intoxicating smell of incense.

Willow leant towards Kyle. "Do you think they can see us?" she whispered.

"With those hoods, I'm not sure they can see anything," Kyle whispered back, "though I wouldn't like to bet on it."

"So wh-what do we do?" said Willow, trying in vain not to sound frightened.

Kyle shrugged. "There's nothing we can do," he said, "except wait – and pray."

Willow said nothing. She understood what he meant. Although the monks were holy men, the atmosphere felt anything but holy. Unlike the reverent tranquillity of a church or cathedral, the glowing circle in the forest felt charged with something bad. Something rotten. Something so immeasurably evil that, in her heart, Willow knew that no prayer she could utter would be powerful enough to keep it at bay.

It was the evil Willow had sensed ever since her first encounter with the Tree of Death. Trembling with foreboding, she looked back.

The tree – if this *was* the same tree – was lying on a long, low wooden cart. At the far end, an immense ball of sacking enclosed the roots. Beside this were a massive hole that had been dug in the ground, and a mound of earth.

"It hasn't been uprooted at all," she said.

Kyle shook his head. "The opposite," he said. "I think we're about to witness its planting, though heavens knows why they waited so long before—"

"Sssh!" said Willow urgently.

Kyle spun round. Walking slowly and solemnly towards the hole in the ground was a short, portly monk who was swinging a brass incense holder to and fro on its chain. Behind him came a second man who, although following, was clearly the more important of the two – the abbot of the monastic order.

He was tall and gaunt and walked with a slight stoop. In his left hand he held a long shepherd's crook made from ebony and silver. In his right hand he carried a box. Unlike all the other monks, his hood was down, and as Kyle and Willow watched him, they noticed something strange.

He had no eyebrows, no beard, and the torch-glow gleamed on his bald scalp. In short, he was completely hairless, and when he blinked, his lashless eyelids quivered like those of a cold-blooded reptile.

Having reached the edge of the pit, the portly monk stopped and dangled the censer over the hole below. The laws of nature demanded that the billowing smoke should rise up and dissipate in the air yet, as Willow and Kyle looked on, the violet clouds grew thicker and heavier, until they coiled down into the hole and sank out of sight. Willow sighed. It was proof – if proof were needed – that natural laws held little sway in this eerie place, with its mournful music and its circle of flame which kept the day at bay.

The tall hairless abbot halted abruptly in front of the tree and raised his arms. Then he drove the crook down into the earth, turned and lifted his head.

"The place is here," he announced. "And the time is now."

The monks fell silent. Their heads remained down.

"We are ready to complete the final undertaking in fulfilment of the ancient prophecy," he proclaimed, and a mournful chorus of "*So be it!*" echoed round the circle of robed figures.

Willow trembled. The monk continued, preaching about the light and darkness, about the seen and the unseen, about power and strength and sacrifice.

The words were strange, yet stranger still was the method of their delivery, for Willow realized that although she could hear his voice and see his lips move, the two did not coincide. It was like watching a foreign film which had been dubbed into English. The words – the *translation* of the words – was inside her head. And Kyle's. And as it continued, the pair of them exchanged quizzical glances. What was it all about?

"The acorn fell," they heard, "as it was always meant to fall. For it was written that the fruit of the oak would drop into the cradle of the one who was destined for eternal greatness.

"And the acorn grew. And the infant grew. Their lives were bound as one.

"When the boy reached the age of eleven, he set out on his own, taking with him nothing but the sapling, depending on the charity of those he met along the way for his survival. Many years he journeyed, many miles he travelled.

"And the sapling grew. And the boy grew, his strength increasing to match the ever heavier tree.

"When the man reached the age of two and twenty, he could no longer carry the tree upon his back. Yet his journey was not yet complete. He sought out others who would help him with his heavy load.

"And the tree grew. And the number of followers grew. And the man ordained these followers into the Order of Marvels.

"This day, the man reached the age of thirty-three. And now, as the prophecy decreed, it is time for man and tree finally to put down roots." He paused, closed his eyes and breathed in deeply.

"And I am the man who was the boy who was the infant. And this," he said, raising his arms in supplication, "is the tree that was the sapling that was the acorn that was there at my birth."

Willow's head spun. There was already too much to take in, and still the hairless abbot had not finished.

"Sanctify! Purify! Ratify!" he bellowed. "The past, the present and all that is to come."

He opened the lid of the box, reached in and pulled out a handful of a powdery substance which he scattered into the pit.

"With the dust of those who bore the tree but perished along the way, the Past shall sanctify the deed. For those who come to the tree shall stay with the tree, for ever." He lay the box down.

"So be it," the monks chanted.

"Be it so," said the abbot.

Out of the corner of her eye, Willow spotted a movement in the circle of monks. She looked round to see a young man and a young woman being ushered towards the pit. Their heads were covered, their feet were bare. The woman was carrying a bundle of rags. As they made their way forward, Willow's heart began pounding. Her legs turned to jelly. She sensed what was going to happen, and there was nothing she could do to prevent it.

The man and woman stopped walking. The abbot – prodigiously strong after a lifetime of carrying the tree – stooped down and scooped them both up in his arms. He raised his head again.

"With these three innocent lives of those who were conceived and born in the shadow of the tree, the Present shall purify the deed. For those who live by the tree shall stay by the tree, for ever."

"So be it," sang the monks.

"Be it so." And with those words, the hairless monk tossed the bodies into the pit. As a pitiful wail echoed from the hole, both Willow and Kyle suddenly understood why he had spoken of three lives, when all they had seen was two. The answer was as simple as it was awful. The bundle of rags was a baby.

Tears streamed down Willow's cheeks. Kyle bit his lower lip but couldn't stop his own eyes from welling up. They had, of course, known that something bad must have happened, but in their wildest dreams they had not imagined that the origins of the Tree of Death could have been so brutal, so monstrous, so wicked.

By now, both Willow and Kyle had come to the conclusion that they could not be seen. Certainly, no one had acknowledged their presence. It was, therefore, all the more petrifying when the abbot did just that.

He spun round abruptly, and they found themselves pinned down by his ferocious stare. His raised arms. His lips moved. It was too late for them to turn and run. The monk's words filled their heads.

"With eyes which have witnessed the everlasting power of the tree, and now behold its creation, so has the Future ratified the deed. Past. Present. Future. The symmetry of time is complete and eternal. For those who discover the tree shall remain with the tree, for ever."

"So be it," came the echoing refrain of the monks.

"Be it so," the reply. The abbot turned away again, pulled the crook from the ground and held it up above his head in triumph. Then he swung it round and pointed it down into the pit.

"The tree shall grow," he roared.

At once the monks laid down their burning torches and hurried towards the tree. Each one knew the precise point on the tree for which he was responsible – this one a branch, that one a section of the trunk. Some looped lengths of rope around the upper branches. Then, together, they lifted the tree up from the cart and waited while ten more carefully unravelled the sacking from around the roots.

When the last of the roots had been released, the monks steered the tree away from the cart, heaved it upright, and lowered it slowly down into the waiting pit.

There was a soft breathy sound, like a sigh of resignation, as the roots sank down into the hole. The baby's cries ceased abruptly.

While half of the band of monks kept the tree standing upright with the taut ropes, the other half set to work refilling the hole. With their bare hands they transferred the mound of earth back into the hole from which it had come. Burying the living. Burying the dead. Anchoring the tree in its final resting place.

Only when they were finished, and the ground around the base of the tree had been trampled flat, were the ropes removed. The monks returned to their burning torches and once again formed their circle of light.

The abbot stood in front of the tree and hung his head. High above him the sky darkened as heavy clouds rolled in overhead and blotted out the rising sun. He touched, in turn, his left temple, his heart, his right temple. Then he fell to his knees and lifted his gaze until he was staring up into the branches.

"In fulfilment of the prophecy I carried you for three and thirty years, turning my back on the evil of the world, and dedicating myself only to your well-being."

"So be it," chanted the monks.

"In fulfilment of the prophecy I have planted you in earth, sanctified by the past, purified by the present and ratified by the future."

"So be it!"

The clouds grew thicker. The sky darkened.

"In fulfilment of the prophecy, a monastery – The Priorie of Marvels – shall be built around your magnificence, that generations shall live and die in your shadow."

"So be it!"

"*Be it so!*" the abbot cried out.

All at once, the sky opened up as if the clouds had been torn in two, and a single lightning bolt hurtled down through the sky. It hissed, it sizzled, it rasped.

"*Now and for ever!*" he proclaimed.

The bolt of lightning struck the abbot square in the chest. He fell forward heavily against the tree, and embraced it as he slid down to the ground. A twist of smoke emerged from the back of his robes. Willow gasped. Kyle stifled a scream. The smell of burning flesh wafted towards them.

The abbot was dead, yet his voice continued. "So shall it begin!" it announced, and Willow and Kyle saw a wispy replica of the abbot rise up from the motionless corpse and sink in to the rough bark of the tree. "*So shall it begin!*"

Suddenly, everything started moving at once. The air sparkled, the leaves of the tree pixellated, and once again Kyle and Willow had the sensation of tumbling forwards down a never-ending tunnel. Circles within circles. Rings within rings.

Cloisters grew up around them, and hooded monks appeared on the tree, nailed, bound, hanging.

The cloisters crumbled. The chapel fell. Steel

glinted as broadswords and scimitars slashed through the air. Monks perished. Soldiers died.

And all the while the forest shifted and changed as trees grew tall, then fell and rotted away, and others took their place. Only the mighty oak, the Tree of Death, remained, growing taller, wider, stronger as the years flashed by.

Men hanging. Women burning. Children, crushed and battered and buried alive. Screams of pain. Death rattle. Victims, victims and more victims. Nameless, unknown victims. Each one perishing in monstrous fulfilment of that ancient prophecy. Each one bound to the tree for eternity.

Amongst the many were those they recognized: Lizzie Greatorex, Tom Marley, Mayor Fothergill, Eddy and Jack Faulkner, Mole.

All at once, and as abruptly as it had begun, so the display of faces came to a halt. Kyle and Willow looked round anxiously. They were standing directly in front of the tree. The familiar tree. The tree with its blackened scar and platform, tied high up in the branches.

"Hello?" came a voice. It was Sara. "Where did you two spring from?" she said.

Willow turned towards her. After all that had taken place, she scarcely dared to believe that normality – her mum cooking, Blue playing, Gary tinkering with the engine of the bus – had really returned. She opened her mouth to speak, but no sound emerged. Sara smiled nervously.

"Are you two OK?" she said. "You look as though you've seen a ghost."

Kyle scratched his head and cleared his throat. "A ghost," he repeated flatly. He reached forward, took Willow's hand in his own and squeezed it tightly. "No," he said. "We haven't seen ... a ghost. Have we, Willow?"

Willow shook her head. Kyle was playing with words – and yet he was right. One ghost alone could never have created the Tree of Death. One ghost alone could never have inspired the degree of fear and foreboding which now overwhelmed the pair of them.

No, it hadn't been one ghost they had seen, but a legion of spirits, too many to count, ensnared down the centuries by the evil tree. And the worst of it all was the terrible discovery that they – Willow and Kyle – were responsible for everything that had happened. For if they hadn't witnessed the abbot's incantations, the cursing of the Tree of Death would never have been successful.

But they had witnessed it. Now it was up to them, and them alone, to break the terrible curse.

18

It was a shock for Kyle and Willow to discover that the meal bubbling over the fire was supper rather than lunch. While they had been trapped in the past, drawn, through their own curiosity, to observe the gory details of the origins of the tree, a whole day had passed. The sun had already disappeared behind the trees.

"You'll stay for something to eat, won't you?" said Sara.

Kyle looked up. He and Willow were sitting next to her tent. He scratched behind his left ear. "That would be nice," he said. "But I ought to tell Mother."

"Oh, I forgot to say," Gary said. "I saw her earlier. She had to get back – something to do with your father. She said she'll see you here tomorrow."

Kyle grinned. "Well, in that case – yes, I'd love something to eat. I'm famished."

"You'd better stick some extra pasta on to boil," said Willow. "A kilo ought to do it."

Kyle laughed, and scratched behind his left ear again. Then his right ear. Then both at the same time, long and hard. "Damn it!" he exclaimed. "I can't stop itching."

"Kyle's got itchy bugs, Kyle's got itchy bugs!" Blue began chanting.

"That's what comes of mixing with riff-raff," said Willow, "though I promise you didn't catch them off me."

"What? You mean..."

"Or me," said Sara, looking up.

"Or me," Gary laughed.

"Not headlice!" said Kyle, wrinkling up his nose in disgust.

Willow lent across and lifted up the hair behind his ears to inspect. Two pale crablike insects scurried for cover. "Fraid so," she said. "And speaking as an expert, I'd say you'd had them for some while. At least a fortnight."

"But I only got home from school on Thursday—" he began.

"Precisely," said Willow. "But then headlice are not known for their respect of privilege."

"I bet I got them off Stinky Jameson," Kyle scowled, "or Harry Creedle ... or Benny Grimshaw." He turned to Willow. "It could have been anyone, couldn't it?"

Willow nodded, happy that it hadn't occurred to him to mention any girls' names. "I wonder how many other boys and girls of Travers College Boarding School have returned home with a little something they weren't expecting for their fees."

"Hmmph!" said Kyle. "So how do you get rid of them?"

"Lygon," said Willow.

"Oh, Willow!" Sara exclaimed. "For heaven's sake."

Willow smirked at Kyle. "It works," she said.

"The stuff's no better than sheep dip," said Sara. "It's full of the most awful chemicals – chemicals proven to cause cancer..." She stood up from the fire. "*And* destroy the central nervous system." She disappeared into the bus, returning a moment later with an old coffee jar filled with a pale green oil. "Try this instead."

Kyle unscrewed the lid and sniffed inside suspiciously. "Pfwooaarr!" he groaned. "What is it?"

"Twenty drops geranium, forty drops bergamot, twenty drops lavender, twenty drops tea tree in one hundred millilitres of vegetable oil," Sara reeled off. "I make it up in bulk. You need to massage it into the scalp and hair, leave it under a shower cap for two hours and then go through your hair with a fine-toothed comb."

"A shower cap?" said Kyle.

"Cling film if you'd prefer," Willow giggled.

Kyle sniffed at the oil a second time. "No, I'm sorry. There is no way I am putting that muck on my head."

"Lygon also causes hair loss," Sara said.

"Now that hasn't been proven," said Willow.

Sara shrugged. "Well, there's one sure way of finding out," she snapped, snatching away the bottle of herbal oil and stomping back to the bus. "Men!" she said at Gary as she passed him. "You're all the same. Stubborn, stupid and vain."

Gary looked up from the engine and laughed. "I wouldn't use it either," he called over to Kyle. "But she's right about the Lygon. It's horrible stuff."

Kyle scratched miserably.

"There's only one way to make sure they go and never come back," said Gary.

"You mean get a haircut like yours?" said Kyle.

Gary turned to Blue. "What's it we say? *A haircut every thirty days...*"

"*Keeps the itchy bugs away!*" Blue cried, and burst out laughing.

"Actually, it's time me and Blue had a trim," said Gary, rubbing his hands on an oily rag. "I'll rig everything up."

"He's got some hair clippers," Willow explained.

Kyle nodded unenthusiastically and scratched his head. Crew-cuts – like white socks, earrings and chewing gum – were plebby according to the pupils at Travers. Any offender was judged to be a "Kevin" until his hair grew again. The itching continued. Kyle scraped at it wildly with his fingernails.

"Aaargh!" he roared. He climbed to his feet, strode over to the bus and sat down on the stool Gary had placed next to the front wheel. "Cut it off," he said. "Cut it all off!"

Willow watched as Gary set to work, flicking an old sheet around Kyle's shoulders, attaching the crocodile-clips to the battery, selecting a comb attachment for the clippers and switching them on. Soon Kyle's thick dark, wavy hair was tumbling down into his lap. Willow smiled to herself. The amiable public school twerp was being transformed into – what was it Kyle's father had said? – an oik!

"Does it look that bad?" said Kyle.

"No, I..." Willow began.

"So why are you laughing?"

"I wasn't. I ... it suits you."

"Hmmph!"

The buzz of the clippers abruptly stopped. "There," said Gary, pulling the sheet away. "You're done."

"Thanks," said Kyle. He stood up, bent over double and rubbed the stray hairs from his head and inside his ears. Then he straightened up and turned to Willow.

"Well?" he said.

"I told you already," said Willow sharply, "so stop fishing for compliments. You need to shampoo it now. There's water in drums at the back of the bus. And when you've done that I'll check through it to make sure it's completely clear."

Kyle looked back at Gary, grinned and shrugged. Then the pair of them spoke at once. "Yes, Mother!" they said and burst out laughing.

Willow screwed her eyes shut with embarrassment. She'd done it again!

By the time Kyle had washed his hair and Willow had gone through it, and Gary had cut Blue's hair and Sara had washed it, and Willow had cut Gary's hair and he had washed it, and Sara (since they were using the water) had washed her hair as well – by the time all of that was done, supper was ready. Sara ladled out the vegetarian sausage and pasta casserole into bowls, Gary poured the drinks, and they all sat down in a circle around the fire, filling their stomachs, slaking their thirst and swapping stories.

Too intent on eating to join in himself, Kyle listened in growing amusement as the conversation shifted from headlice and tapeworms, through scars and birthmarks, to verrucas, blackheads and boils. He'd never heard anything like it at a mealtime before. Not at Travers and certainly never at home.

He was seventeen years old, but he realized he was sniggering like a naughty six-year-old.

He glanced round at Willow, to share his laughter with her, to tell her how much he liked her family. But Willow was not laughing. It had grown dark without his noticing, and the firelight, flickering on her face, made her look tired, drawn, and oddly vulnerable. He leant over and wrapped his hand around hers.

Willow looked up. She smiled bravely, but Kyle noticed her lower lip trembling. "I'm frightened," she whispered.

"We'll be all right," said Kyle.

"I mean, I've been trying really hard," she went on, "ever since we got back, but..." She swallowed. "I can't forget *that*," she said, jerking her head back to the ominous tree which lurked behind them in the shadows. "What we saw. What it did. What it's going to do..."

"We'll be all right," Kyle said again, as if simply repeating it would make it true.

Willow shifted round and kissed his cheek. "You're so sweet," she said. Kyle winced. Sweet? He hated the word "sweet". It was the kiss-of-death word, the thanks-but-no-thanks word. When a girl called you sweet it meant she liked you, but as a friend and no more. Willow laughed. "Especially when you're blushing," she said, and kissed him again.

"Yuck!" said Blue.

Gary laughed. "I take it you'll be sleeping in Willow's tent, Kyle?" he said.

Kyle went even redder.

Gary licked his index finger, pointed it at Kyle and pretended to touch it to his burning face. "Sssssss!" he hissed, imitating a droplet of water splashing down on a hot-plate. And everybody – including Kyle – laughed.

"And talking of sleeping arrangements," Gary went on, "I've decided to sleep up on the platform."

"But—" Sara began.

"No, don't try and stop me," said Gary. "I've got no more problems with the vertigo."

"But—" Sara said again.

"And I *know* the evictions aren't supposed to start till Thursday, but I don't trust them. I reckon they could come at any time now."

Willow and Kyle exchanged glances. They felt disloyal keeping the information they had to themselves.

"But..." said Sara for a third time, and stopped.

Gary looked at her. "What?" he said.

"That's just so typical of you," she said crossly. "You make plans for yourself without ever asking me what I might like to do." Gary stared at her, perplexed. "You see," Sara went on, "it never even occurred to you that I might want to spend the night up on the platform."

"Well, do you?"

"Yes!"

Gary raised his eyes to the skies. "OK," he said, "we can both sleep up there."

"And what about Blue?" said Sara. "Do we leave him to sleep in the bus on his own? He's still only three."

Gary shrugged. "He could sleep up there as well."

"He could not," Sara snapped. "It's far too dangerous."

Willow looked from Gary to Sara and back again as the bickering continued. There they were, the pair of them, both vying for a place up in the evil tree. Neither of them had the remotest idea what they were letting themselves in for. Suddenly she realized they were both staring at her.

"Well?" said Sara.

"Well, what?" she said.

"Which one of us do *you* think should get to sleep on the platform?"

Willow gulped. It was the dilemma of the hot-air balloon all over again. For the second time in her life Willow had to choose between them – Sara and Gary. Which one should she condemn to a night with the Tree of Death? The answer, of course, was neither.

"Kyle and I are going to sleep up there," she said, turning to Kyle. "Aren't we?"

186

Kyle nodded unenthusiastically. "Yeah," he said. He looked at Sara and Gary. "If that's OK. Only I might not be here tomorrow night."

Gary nodded. "You go ahead," he said.

"But it's my turn tomorrow," said Sara.

Willow smiled grimly. If everything went as planned, the tree would be gone by then. She climbed to her feet, stretched and yawned. "Come on," she said to Kyle. "Help me get the stuff from the tent."

It was too hot inside the individual sleeping bags – that was Willow's excuse – so she had unzipped them both and laid them out on the rubber mattress-rolls, one on top of the other. They lay between them, wrapped in each other's arms. A hurricane lamp glowed dimly from a nearby branch. An owl hooted. Willow sat up on her elbow and stroked Kyle's hair.

"It does suit you," she said. "You look like a big teddy bear."

Kyle groaned. It sounded as bad as "sweet". Worse. He was about to tell her as much when Willow spoke again.

"We *are* doing the right thing, aren't we?" she said.

"What do you mean?" said Kyle.

"Trying to make sure the tree gets cut down," she whispered, as if trying to keep it a secret from the tree itself. "I mean, it's so old, so beautiful..."

Kyle looked at her as if she were mad. "Of course we are," he said, and quoted once again the final line from Lizzie Greatorex's verse. "*So long it stands, so long shall the Death Knell toll.*"

Willow sighed, lay back and stared up into the shadowy depths of its branches. A warm breeze rustled through the leaves. The owl hooted again.

"The oak tree has been cursed," he said. "We both saw it, and we both know the consequences. Those who come to the tree shall stay with the tree, for ever," he said.

"For ever," Willow repeated drowsily.

"Victim after victim. Death after death," said Kyle. "For ever."

"For ever."

"And if the tree *is* destroyed," he said, "maybe all those spirits which have been captured by the tree will finally be released. Find peace. Find rest... Willow?"

He shifted round and looked at her. Her eyes were closed and her breathing was slow and regular. He pulled aside a strand of hair from her lips and snuggled up.

"Night-night, Willow," he whispered. "Sweet dreams. See you in the morning." An icy shudder tingled up and down his spine. "I hope," he added.

19

The night passed quietly, uneventfully. The moon rose and fell and, as far as they were aware, neither Kyle nor Willow had any dreams, sweet or otherwise. It was only later, when the sun came up, that their eyelids started flickering. Kyle dreamt he was with his father watching Formula 1 cars speeding endlessly round a race-track, lap after lap. Willow dreamt she was stroking Arthur, her pet guinea pig. The poor creature was obviously terribly confused. Not only was it giving birth to six, seven, eight tiny guinea piglets, but it was purring like a cat. *Prrr ... rrr ... rrr ... rrr*. Louder than the hum of the fridge. Louder than the drone of traffic. Louder and louder.

PRRR ... RRR ... RRR ... RRR ... Like a heavy engine revving.

Willow sat bolt upright. "Kyle!" she cried out. "They're coming!"

"Wh-what?" said Kyle. The racing cars disappeared. He looked round, bleary-eyed.

"It's the eviction and demolition crews," said Willow. "They're here."

Instantly wide awake, Kyle was up. "You're right," he said.

As he spoke, the first of a line of heavy vehicles came into view. It was a bulldozer, bucket down, clearing a path before it. Two more bulldozers came after, followed by a truck, a van and two cherry pickers, all lumbering through the forest like steel dinosaurs. Last in the line was a tractor. Green, squat and trundling along on caterpillar treads, it looked just like a tank – the only difference being that instead of a gun at the front, there was a chainsaw.

"Quick! Let's get the chains on," said Willow. "We've got to make this look real."

They padlocked themselves into place, threw away the keys and checked down below them. The first bulldozer had made it to the tree. The driver had stopped, climbed out of his cab, and was calling over to a second man who had climbed down from the truck. With his suit, clipboard and mobile, he seemed to be in charge.

"We'll leave it for now," Willow heard him

shouting above the chugging of the engines. "My orders are to concentrate on the occupied trees," he said. "We remove the occupants and cut down the tree so they can't return."

"Right-o!" the bulldozer-driver shouted.

Willow watched in horror as the man climbed back into his cab. It was all about to go horribly wrong. They couldn't leave without cutting down the Tree of Death, they just couldn't! She leant over the railing and, patting her flattened palm to her mouth, whooped like a Red Indian. Kyle joined in. The man in the suit spun round. He looked up, scribbled something on his clipboard and issued new orders.

While the other vehicles were to continue on up to Crow's Nest Camp, one of the cherry pickers and the chainsaw tractor would remain, to evict the protesters and fell the tree.

"Yes!" Willow muttered under her breath.

"Willow! Kyle!" they heard a moment later. It was Sara and Gary, woken at last by the disturbance outside.

"Are you all right up there?" said Sara. "What's going on?"

"They've arrived early, is what," said Gary angrily, "just like I said they would."

Blue bounded off to look at the giant machines, and whistled in awe (as best as he could) as they rumbled past.

"Right, you two," the man in the suit called up. "Why don't you just come down quietly?"

"So that you can destroy this magnificent tree?" Sara cried out. "A tree which has stood here for hundreds of years. A tree which has seen the Dark Ages and the Enlightenment. That was here during the War of the Roses and the Battle of Trafalgar, that survived two world wars. And you want to just chop it down in the next five minutes? Over my dead body!" she yelled furiously. "Willow! Kyle!" she called. "You stay put."

As the man spoke into his mobile, the van – which had been following the others through the clearing – abruptly stopped. Three policemen jumped out and ran back towards the tree. Two of them grabbed Sara. The third cautioned Gary not to do anything silly. Blue, who was now conducting the chainsaw tractor with a stick as it split off from the line of vehicles, had not noticed the cherry picker rolling towards him.

"Blue!" Gary screamed. He shrugged off the policeman and raced towards his son. "Blue! Blue!"

Willow stared down. She saw it all in an instant: Gary, the policeman, Blue, with his back turned, the cherry picker getting closer. "Not Blue!" she murmured desperately. "Not Baby Blue!" If she could, she would have leapt from the platform and dragged him from the path of the oncoming vehicle. But the clanking chains reminded her that this was not possible.

"Blue!" she screamed. "Get out of there! BLUE!"

Half a dozen metres away from the boy, Gary was tripped up by a concealed loop of tree root and came crushing down to the ground. For an awful moment Willow thought the policeman was going to pin him down to stop him running away. But no. He'd seen Blue, too. Ignoring Gary, he raced on and threw himself into the air, grabbed the boy and rolled over into a bank of bracken.

The cherry picker rumbled over the spot where Blue had been standing. Blue sat up, looked round and burst into tears.

"My stick," he howled. "It's broke."

Willow stared down at the stick that Blue had been using as his conductor's baton, and shivered. It was broken in several pieces. She sighed. The tree had almost claimed another victim. And when the men came to remove her (one climbing up the tree from below and one coming in from the front on the cherry picker) all she could feel was relief — relief that Blue was still alive, relief that she and Kyle were about to leave the evil tree.

One by one, the men cut through the chains with heavy cable-cutters and bundled first Willow and then Kyle on to the cherry picker. Neither of them offered more than token resistance, the little they did show being for Gary and Sara's benefit.

As the cherry picker swung round and lowered them to the ground, the driver of the chainsaw tractor climbed back into his cab. He pressed a button and the engine chugged. He flicked a switch and the chainsaw whined. Then he pushed a lever. The tractor lurched forward until the chainsaw was level with the tree.

"No!" wailed Sara, tears streaming down her face. "You mustn't. You can't!"

The driver turned the steering wheel sharply to the left. The chainsaw screamed as it bit into the wood, and sent a spray of dark brown chips of bark flying through the air.

"Yes!" Willow whispered. It was happening. The Tree of Death, which had brought about the destruction of so many lives, was itself finally being destroyed.

The next moment, she realized she had celebrated too soon. With a whooping and whistling, a group of protesters came racing down into the clearing and linked arms in a circle around the tree. The tractor driver stopped the engine and stilled the chainsaw. A girl pushed a rose into the gap between the chain and blade.

Then the police reinforcements appeared. They came from over the ridge and from the woods to the north-west, in a pincer movement. Each one was in full riot gear, with shield, helmet and rubber truncheon. Some had dogs. Some were armed with rifles loaded with rubber bullets. Some carried canisters of tear-gas.

"Here we go again," Willow said softly.

The two sides faced each other, like a phalanx of musk ox against a pack of advancing wolves. It was stalemate. But not for long. Under strict instructions to ensure the success of the eviction, the police advanced and waded into the circle.

Suddenly, Willow became aware of someone standing behind her. She spun round. A man in a dark suit was standing there. "Who are you?" she demanded.

The man smiled. "Kyle, perhaps you'd like to introduce us."

Kyle looked away awkwardly. "Willow," he said "this is Rodney Bickley. My father's friend."

"The Under Sheriff," Willow said with as much venom in her voice as she could muster.

The man chuckled. "I'm not quite sure what inspired you to give us the information you did, young lady," he said, "but we were very grateful for it." He turned to walk away. "Very grateful indeed," he called back over his shoulder.

Willow looked round her anxiously. What if someone had seen the three of them talking? What would they think? Things happened to those who collaborated with the enemy, and there was no way she could ever explain why she wanted this particular tree destroyed. All she could do was hope that no one had noticed.

Thankfully, she thought it unlikely. With the battle in full swing, everyone looked far too engrossed in their own business to have noticed her and the Under Sheriff together.

In front of her, the scuffles were increasing both in number and intensity. Voices were being raised, fists clenched and punches thrown. Truncheon blows rained down indiscriminately. She saw a man in a green vest and army fatigues fall to one side and gash his head on a rock. The next moment a policeman was felled by a blow to the back of his neck. It was struck by the girl with the rose, only now she was carrying one of the logs Gary had chopped up for the fire.

Willow and Kyle simply stood and stared, horrified yet unsurprised by the violence being unleashed beneath the tree. It was, after all, no more than could be expected. Ever since the day that it had been cursed, the Tree of Death had always caused death and injury to those who strayed within its circle of influence.

It was difficult to guess how many victims the tree might have claimed that day if the driver of the chainsaw tractor hadn't acted as he did. Taking matters into his own hands, he locked the doors on both sides of the cab, pressed the button, flicked the switch and pushed the lever forward.

The screaming blade shredded the rose in an instant, and proceeded to rip into the trunk. The brown chips of bark turned creamy white as the chainsaw tore into the wood itself.

The protesters went wild. Some of them hammered furiously on the sides of the tractor. Others tried to jam the blade with anything they could lay their hands on – rocks, logs, bundles of cloth – yet all in vain. The police, while shouting at the driver to switch off the saw, used the opportunity to arrest those temporarily off guard.

Ignoring the cries of police and protesters alike, the driver locked the steering wheel on full left turn and accelerated. The chainsaw screamed and woodchips fanned out into the air. Gathering together on one side, the protesters began pushing at the tractor.

"Heave-HO!" they roared. "Heave-HO!"

The tractor began to rock backwards and forwards, a little further with each push. The driver clung on to his seat grimly. The policemen tried to pull them away. And all the while the scream of the chainsaw grew louder and louder.

"We've got to get all these people back," Willow heard a policeman shouting, "before the tree..." He fell silent.

Before the tree does what? Willow wondered. Falls? Kills someone? She glanced round and, like the policeman, like the driver, like Kyle, she gasped with amazement.

The entire tree was lit up by a dazzling blue light, as if it had been charged up with some electrical force.

In twos and threes, protesters and policemen noticed what was happening. They abandoned their struggle with one another, and united to help their injured companions away from the treacherous tree. Sparking, crackling, hissing, it hurled jagged bolts of blinding light from its fingered branches and down at the ground below.

And still the chainsaw screamed, and still the wood chips flew as, little by little, the trunk was cut through.

A policeman standing directly in front of Willow and Kyle was struck by a bolt of the curious electricity. He clutched at his chest and went down like a stone. The electrical charge glowed all round his body as he lay on the ground, frothing, twitching. A second policeman and one of the protesters tried to drag him away to safety. Kyle dashed forward to help and together the three of them pulled him clear and propped him up against a rock out of reach of the bolts of energy. There he sat, eyes shot blood-red and staring, and hair standing on end.

"I got an electric shock when I touched him," Kyle told Willow when he got back to her.

Willow nodded. "Some kind of awful power is being unleashed," she said. "And look where it's centred."

Kyle turned and stared in front of him. With the area directly around the tree now clear of people, the bolts of electricity were all concentrated on the one subject which was still threatening the safety of the ancient tree: the chainsaw tractor.

The vehicle was glowing as if white-hot, and vibrating furiously as a continous stream of blinding electric energy poured down on it from the tree. The windows had misted up inside, but through them the fuzzy silhouette of the driver could still be seen hunched up over the steering wheel.

All at once, there was a resounding crash as the glass exploded. Willow and Kyle saw the driver glance round, wide-eyed with terror, as though realizing for the first time the predicament he was in.

For a moment he remained motionless. Then, as if suddenly reaching a decision, he reached over into the box beside him, selected something from it, and disappeared from view below. The next moment he sprang back up and leapt through the glassless window. He landed heavily, but scrambled to his feet at once and made a desperate stumbling dash for the cover of the surrounding undergrowth. There, he collapsed. Willow and Kyle raced round to meet him.

"Are you all right?" said Willow, crouching down beside him.

The man looked up. With his long red hair sticking out from beneath his yellow hard-hat, he looked like a clown. He nodded. "Think so," he said.

Kyle offered his hand and helped the man to his feet. "How come the engine's still running?" he asked.

The man grinned. "Jammed a jemmy under the accelerator, din'I?" he said, proudly. "Keep the pressure on the saw." Willow stared at the man in amazement. What had made him act so courageously, so selflessly? Had he, too, lost someone to the tree? Was he seeking revenge? Or was he simply a good man who had sensed the evil within the tree and knew it must be destroyed. "After all," he added, "didn't want to lose my bonus, did I?"

"Bonus?" said Willow incredulously.

"Get a bonus for every occupied tree we cut down, don' we?" said the man, grinning stupidly.

She turned away in disgust. She wanted to shout at him for his lack of principles. She wanted to tell him how much she hated people like him, and the Under Sheriff, and the police – people who eased their conscience about destroying the environment by claiming that they were "only doing their job". She wanted to say so much, yet she bit her tongue and remained silent. From experience, Willow knew that men like the driver were impervious to criticism – and anyway, with the Tree of Death, hadn't the driver done exactly what she wanted?

Just then a cry of terror erupted from a group of protesters standing in a huddle to Willow's left. She saw their open-mouthed terror, their wild-eyed horror, but what had frightened them so?

"Look!" Kyle screamed. "Over there!"

Willow followed his pointing finger. There *was* something there, though what, she couldn't say. It was white and wispy. It darted this way and that, snaking round and between the terrified onlookers. Suddenly, it was joined by a second, and then a third. And on the far side of the clearing, another group of protesters and police were also crying out with fear.

"They're coming from the cut in the tree trunk," Kyle said.

Willow nodded. The chainsaw had by now cut through more than half of the trunk. "They must be – aaaaargh!" she screamed as one of the wispy white apparitions emerged from the tree, twirled in the air, and launched itself directly at her and Kyle.

A ghostly head and shoulders loomed up before them, flew off behind their backs and reappeared in front. The face grimaced, grinned and was gone again.

"It's a ghost!" Willow gasped. "The ghost of one of the victims of the tree."

Kyle nodded.

The air filled with more and more of the comet-like spirits. They danced. They spiralled. They swooped and dived.

"The spirits are being set free," said Willow, a broad smile spreading over her face. She threw her arms around Kyle and squeezed him tightly. "We've released them. We've done it! We've—"

BOOOOM!

The blast was as powerful as it was unexpected. It lifted Willow and Kyle off the ground and tossed them backwards through the air. They landed heavily on their backs, and lay there, winded and scared.

Kyle was the first to stir. He climbed to his feet, he helped Willow up, and the pair of them squinted into the billowing clouds of dust where the tree had been.

Apart from the ringing in their ears, the forest was silent. The tractor engine had stopped running, and the chainsaw was still. Slowly, the dust settled. As it did so, the scene before them was gradually revealed. It filled Willow with despair.

"Oh, no!" she groaned.

The tractor and chainsaw lay scattered around the clearing in various pieces. The electrical force must have short-circuited the electrics or ignited the fuel tank – at any rate, the chainsaw tractor had been completely destroyed. Whereas the tree – the evil Tree of Death – had not.

There it stood, as tall as before, as dark as before, yet infinitely more menacing than either she or Kyle had ever seen it. For there, nailed to its trunk and hanging from its branches like some demonic harvest, were all the spirits that had ever died there. Each one was in precisely the place where he or she had been at the moment of death. A wailing and a soft moaning whispered through the air.

"Oh, Kyle!" Willow gasped. "What have we done?"

Kyle reached out and took her hand. "We did our best," he said.

Willow sniffed. The spirits writhed and squirmed horribly. "But our best just wasn't good enough, was it?" she said.

"No," said Kyle softly. "No, it... Hang on!" He looked round. "What was that?"

"What?" said Willow. "I can't—"

"Ssssh!" said Kyle, and cocked his head to one side. And there it was again. A soft, squeaky, creaking noise. "*That*," he said.

Willow listened. The creaking sound came again and again, slightly louder each time. It was, she realized, coming from directly in front of her. From the centre of the clearing.

"It's the tree!" she bellowed. "It's falling."

"Stand back!" several voices shouted.

This way and that way the tree swayed, backwards and forwards like a giant metronome. The creaking grew louder still – and then abruptly stopped. Willow held her breath. The next moment, the air was torn by the sound of ear-splitting splintering.

"She's coming down!" somebody yelled.

The tree lurched and twisted – and toppled down through the air with a loud WHOOOOSH! It crashed to the ground. The earth trembled. Then all was still, as a sudden sense of peace and tranquillity descended over the whole clearing.

It was all Willow could do to stop herself whooping for joy. The tree had been destroyed. And, as she and Kyle looked on, the spirits – released this time for ever – left their places of torment and spiralled upwards into the sky in a rainbow of wonderful colours, off and away.

She turned and hugged Kyle. Tears were streaming down her face. Anyone watching might have supposed they were tears of grief for the felling of the tree. Only she and Kyle knew what they really were – tears of joy.

Tom Marley, Lizzie Greatorex, Eddy and Jack – all the victims of the accursed tree would find peace at last.

All round the clearing the protesters and police

were standing in open-mouthed shock. Incredulous. Transfixed. No one quite dared to trust their senses, no one was prepared to talk about what they had just experienced until someone else did first.

Willow walked slowly towards the stump of the tree. Kyle followed her. Together they looked down at the countless concentric circles – the rings within rings – across the severed trunk. Each one represented a year of the tree's life. Many – too many – were scarred with the tragedies that had occurred.

"Tom Marley must have been hanged about here," Willow said, pointing to a couple of the rings.

"And Lizzie Greatorex must have been burned about here," said Kyle, moving his finger closer to the centre of the tree.

"And here," said Willow, finding the thirty-third ring out from the centre, "is when the tree was planted. And cursed."

Kyle stood up and rested his hands on her shoulders. "Come on," he said. "Let's go. It's all over now."

"Is it?" came a voice, nasal and sneering. "Is it really?"

Willow spun round, terrified for a split second to find herself confronted with the hairless abbot. "Oh, it's you," she said. "What do you want?"

Sleaze wiped his mouth on his sleeve and looked at her through hooded eyes. "Interesting friends you got," he said.

"Do you mean me?" Kyle said, thrusting his head forward into Sleaze's smug face.

"You? Interesting?" he whined. He turned back to Willow. "I meant the Under Sheriff," he said. "A certain Mr Blickley."

"Bickley," said Willow automatically.

"Oh, so you *do* know him," said Sleaze. "I think quite a lot of people would be very interested to know the reason why you do. And," he added, "precisely what the information was that he was so grateful for."

Kyle had had enough. He jumped up, grabbed Sleaze by the front of his shirt and dragged him up off the ground. "Listen to me, you horrible little squit—"

"No, Kyle," said Willow, tugging at his clenched fist. "Let him go. He can say what he likes. I don't care. My conscience is clear."

Kyle released his grip. Sleaze stumbled and fell to the ground. Willow glared down at him.

After all she'd been through – the nightmares, the visions, the terrifying events that had unfolded – there was slimy Sleaze, of all people, daring to question her motives. But it was over now. Completely over. She remembered that last sight of the rainbow spirits as they disappeared into the heavens for ever, and her lips broke into a smile.

"My conscience is clear," she said again. "Absolutely clear." She turned to Kyle. "Hurry up. If we're going to stop any more trees being felled, we'd better get up to Crow's Nest Camp as quickly as we can."

Kyle laughed. "The way I feel just now, I reckon we could do just about anything."

As he watched Willow and Kyle walk off together, hand in hand, Sleaze screwed his finger into his temple. "Bonkers," he muttered. "Stark, staring bonkers, the pair of them."

Certainly Willow and Kyle were feeling strange. With the threat of the tree suddenly gone, they both felt giddy with relief, lightheaded with success. It was as if a huge heavy rucksack had been lifted from their shoulders.

"We did it!" Willow kept repeating as they waded through the bracken, and on up the hill. They passed over a clump of limp wild garlic. The whole circle had wilted, and Willow kicked triumphantly at the dead leaves. "We really, really did it!"

Kyle laughed. "We certainly did," he said.

Willow shook her head. "I still can't believe it," she said. "All those people. All those real, historical people—"

"They're all fine now," Kyle reminded her. "Everything is. Like you said. We did it."

They stopped and turned and faced one another. They kissed each other greedily. They fell down on to the soft, springy mattress of fallen leaves.

"You and me, Willow," whispered Kyle. "You and me."

20

When they finally arrived at Crow's Nest Camp later that hot Monday morning in August, Willow and Kyle discovered that everything was even better than they could ever have hoped. Not only had the evil Tree of Death fallen, not only had its victims' spirits been released, but news of the exploding tractor had already got through and the men were refusing – bonus or no bonus – to cut down any more trees.

What was more, despite interference caused by the electrical force around the tree, an amateur film-maker had managed to capture several minutes of film of the tree shortly before it fell. On the television news that night, viewers were spellbound by the sight of the ancient oak covered in fuzzy spectral lights which, as the tree fell, flew off into the sky.

Scientists dismissed the pictures as footage of a freak electrical charge brought about by the area of exceptionally high atmospheric pressure, and certainly the violent thunderstorms which followed soon after seemed to confirm this. However, no one listened to the scientists. As far as Joe Public was concerned, the film proved once and for all that ghosts or spirits – call them what you will – really did exist. And it was this fact that finally saved Marvis Ridge from destruction.

Ironically – given the evil that had been worked there – because of the existence of the ancient monastery, the land around the Ridge was deemed to be hallowed ground and planning permission for the by-pass was withdrawn. Instead, the costlier yet environmentally friendlier tunnel scheme was implemented. For once, the protesters had scored a victory.

With their campaign successfully concluded, the travellers left Marvis Ridge. Some of them went west to protest about a proposed motorway widening in Pendell's Marsh. Some drove north to express their opposition to the building of a second runway at O'Donnell Airport. One of their number, however, remained.

Willow had at last decided to leave Sara, Blue and Gary. Sleaze had tried to spread rumours about her and the Under Sheriff, but since the outcome of the protest had been so successful, no one had listened to him. However, that was not the reason for her remaining in Bridgemorton. She stayed because of Kyle.

It was Mrs Montcrieff who, having talked her husband round to the idea, suggested she move in to the White House. Willow, of course, leapt at the chance. Not only would she be able to be with Kyle, but finally she would regain what she had lost so many years earlier – a roof over her head. Her life on the road was at an end.

As the long summer vacation drew to a close, Willow enrolled on a course at the nearby Listcombe College. So did Kyle. Faced with the choice between Willow and Travers, he had chosen the former. Naturally, Mr Montcrieff had been outraged, but, having ranted and raved, he finally came round – just as Mrs Montcrieff had assured them he would.

Kyle and Willow were now officially an item. Even Mr Montcrieff could see that his son was happier than he had ever known him before. "Just make sure you don't flunk your exams," he told them.

"We won't," they promised.

Shortly before the start of the new term, Kyle bought a small second-hand car. Buses into Listcombe were notoriously unreliable and it meant they no longer had to rely on Mrs Montcrieff for lifts. More importantly, it gave them an extra hour in bed each morning.

As the academic year continued, they thought less and less about the haunted oak tree. Apart from their studies, Kyle played rugby for the college and boxed at a local club, while Willow raised money for CrisisAid and took up T'ai Chi. They were always busy. It was only when the tunnel opened – a year to the day after the felling of the oak tree – that the awful events that had taken place the previous summer up on Marvis Ridge came back to them.

Although Willow had a room of her own, she spent most of her time up in the Megabase with Kyle. They were both there when news of the tunnel opening came on the radio.

"It'll make the journey to college a lot quicker," said Kyle.

Willow nodded, but made no reply. She was working on the computer, putting the finishing touches to an essay. Kyle was pedalling furiously on his exercise bike.

"Should be able to make it there in fifteen minutes," he panted. "Door to door."

"Uh-huh," Willow mumbled.

"Rather than fifty minutes," he added. "Or even an hour when the traffic's particularly bad."

Willow sat back in her chair. "Kyle!" she said. "I'm trying to get this finished."

Kyle stopped pedalling. "I know," he said. "Only..."

Willow grinned. She knew what Kyle was like. He wouldn't be happy until he had driven through the tunnel for himself. Come to that, neither would she. After all, if it hadn't been for them, the tunnel would never have been built in the first place. "Come on, then," she laughed. "Let's try it out."

Five minutes later they were speeding out of Bridgemorton on to the ring-road, following the new signs for *Listcombe via Marvis Tunnel*. The road disappeared into the hill just north of Frog Corner.

"Wheeee!" Willow squealed as they entered the tunnel.

It was long, curved and lined with concrete. Bright lights alternated with huge fans along the arched roof. It was hard to imagine that far above this slice of twentieth-century technology was Marvis Ridge itself, where people had walked for thousands of years and where a certain accursed oak tree – the Tree of Death – had wreaked such havoc.

Kyle put his foot down. "Make that *ten* minutes," he said, as the tunnel curved to the left. "I reckon we... *Aaaagh!*" he screamed in sudden terror.

"No!" Willow cried out, and raised her arms defensively. "*No!*"

Kyle braked. The wheels skidded. The car spun.

Yet the hideous apparition which had materialized remained fixed in front of the windscreen.

Tall, gaunt and completely hairless, it hovered behind the glass, leering menacingly. Its reptile eyes glowed a fiery red, and, as its black forked tongue flickered in and out, so blinding bolts of electricity rained down on the car.

The bodywork glowed, white hot. The steering wheel trembled. The tyres burned.

Willow squeezed her eyes shut. Kyle held his breath. As the car hurtled towards the side wall, the creature's thin, cruel lips parted.

"So shall it begin again," the voice proclaimed. "For, as it was spoken, those who discover the tree shall remain with the tree. For ever."

Point Horror Unleashed

CALLING ALL POINT HORROR FANS!

Welcome to the new wave of fear. If you were scared before, you'll be *terrified* now...

Transformer
Philip Gross

Look into the eyes of the night...

The Carver
Jenny Jones

The first cut is the deepest...

Blood Sinister
Celia Rees

Cursed be he who looks inside...

At Gehenna's Door
Peter Beere

Abandon hope...

House of Bones
Graham Masterton

Home, sweet home...

The Vanished
Celia Rees

Come and play, come and *play*...

Look out for:
Catchman
Chris Wooding

Point Horror Unleashed.
It's one step beyond...